Skindeep
Toeckey Jones

1 8 1 7

HARPER & ROW, PUBLISHERS

Cambridge, Philadelphia, San Francisco, London, Mexico City, São Paolo, Singapore, Sydney

NEW YORK

Skindeep

Copyright © 1986 by Toeckey Jones

Designed by Joyce Hopkins

1 2 3 4 5 6 7 8 9 10

First Edition

Library of Congress Cataloging-in-Publication Data
Jones, Toeckey.
  Skindeep.

  "A Charlotte Zolotow book"
  Summary: Living in a society where racial prejudice
is actually part of the national law, South African
teenager Rhonda is stunned by a secret from her
boyfriend's past.
  [1. South Africa—Fiction.   2. Prejudices—Fiction]
I. Title.
PZ7.J7275Sk 1986   [Fic]   85-45843
ISBN 0-06-023051-7
ISBN 0-06-023052-5 (lib. bdg.)

For my mother and Chris,
and any real-life Daves
in South Africa.
And also for Margaret,
with gratitude.

Skindeep

one

first person

It was Dave's shaved head that first made me notice him. Lynn and I spotted him simultaneously, as soon as he entered the canteen.

"Hey, look," she said, shoving me in the ribs with her elbow. "Here comes Kojak."

We both stared at the conspicuously odd figure who was now pushing his way through the congestion of students milling round the entrance. I was aware of one or two people at other tables also staring at him as he joined the queue in front of the service counter.

Lynn nudged me again. "Fancy him, Rhond?"

"Don't be ridiculous," I told her.

"You know what they say about bald men—they're supposed to be more virile."

3

"That's a lot of baloney."

"Maybe," she said.

I gazed round the canteen, searching for the Handsome Hulk who had attracted my attention the day before. He had been sitting at a table in the corner; but he wasn't sitting there today, or anywhere else that I could see. With a growing sense of disappointment, I checked the room once more, slowly and methodically.

"Who're you looking for?" asked Lynn.

"Nobody."

Half rising, she peered about, trying to discover the source of my interest. Suddenly she ducked down and grasped my arm.

"Guess what? Don't look now, but Kojak's giving you the eye. I think he fancies you. Should I beckon him to come and join us?"

"Just you dare!" I warned her.

Irritably, I reached for a cigarette, then changed my mind and pushed the packet away. I was smoking too much; if I wasn't careful I would become hooked on the habit. Lynn had left her chair to chat with someone she knew at the next table. The general noise level was too loud for me to hear what she was saying. For want of anything better to do, I inspected my nail varnish.

After a moment, however, I couldn't resist glancing towards the service counter. Baldie had progressed along it as far as the cash register, where he was standing with a tray, waiting for his change. He wasn't even facing in my direction. He was contemplating the shelves of sweets and cigarettes and stationery on the wall above the cashier's head. I checked down the line of students behind him. The Handsome Hulk wasn't among them.

Blast! I had been so sure he would turn up today. After all, he had kept looking at me yesterday, and once, catching my eye, he had even vaguely smiled. If only I had smiled back, then perhaps he would have come over and . . . Blast! Why did I have to be so slow off the mark? Next time, dammit, I would encourage him. I would smile first, invitingly—

My expression froze. Baldie was staring at me and I realized I had smiled straight at him in my reverie. I dipped my head, cursing silently. Now Baldie would think I was trying to encourage *him*. Well, if that's what he thought, he was in for a nasty surprise. I would sooner drop dead than acknowledge such an obvious weirdo.

I kept my head down. Peering through my hair, I saw that he was making his way towards my table. If he said anything to me, I would ignore him, I decided.

"Excuse me, do you mind if I sit here?"

He had a surprisingly pleasant voice. I almost looked up, but I repressed the impulse. He cleared his throat. Then Lynn appeared and he repeated his question to her.

"Sure," she said. "Help yourself."

She ignored my glare and cleared a space on the table for his tray. He thanked her and sat down. I could feel his eyes on me. I was compelled, finally, to look up. His irises were an extraordinary translucent greenish gold.

He said something to me.

"Wh-at?" I stuttered.

"I'm Dave."

The outline of his face and hairless skull came back into focus. Lynn spoke to him.

"She's Rhonda. I'm Lynn."

He was silent, still looking at me.

"Hey, tell us." Lynn leaned closer to him. "I'm curious to know, why do you shave your head?"

At last he turned away, towards her. "What makes you so sure I shave it?"

"Ag, come on now, you can see it's shaved. You're not bald. So?"

"So?"

"So tell us, or don't you want—"

"To get rid of the lice," he said matter-of-factly, and he stirred his coffee and began to drink it.

Lynn and I both gaped at him. I inspected him closely from the face down. He looked clean enough and so did his clothes. His bright green-and-orange-patterned pullover reflected an unusual amber luminosity in his eyes as his gaze intercepted mine. My face went hot. Tight-lipped, I frowned down at the crumbs on my plate.

"You're putting me on," Lynn decided. "You know, you'd look sexy with curls—don't you think he'd look sexy with curls, Rhond? Hey, is your hair curly, Dave?"

His whole body became rigid, and for an awful instant I thought he was going to be violent. The cup he was holding jerked; then he put it down very carefully.

"It's none of your effing business."

Lynn, for once, was temporarily speechless. He glanced across at me. Our eyes met for only a split second, but something I glimpsed in his expression—a strange, haunted look—cut me to the quick.

"I'm sorry," said Lynn. "I was just joking. I'm sorry. . . . Okay?"

"Okay." His grin had the effect of a burst of sunshine breaking through a heavy cloud bank. He picked up his hot dog and held it out towards Lynn as if it were a peace offering. "Want a bite?"

With an affectedly coy gesture, she removed the gum from her mouth and took a tiny nibble off the end of the roll. Then she made some comment that I didn't catch. He laughed.

"Would *you* like a bite?" he asked me.

I shook my head stiffly as Lynn made a further remark in a suggestive undertone. They were both laughing now. Dragging my hair forward, I began combing through the ends in search of tangles. I was annoyed; with Lynn because she was flirting with him, and with him because I knew he was watching me out of the side of his eye.

Trust my luck! I told myself sourly. *It's just the bloody same old story all over again.* So much for the supposed advantages of being blond. Lynn, who was plump and prone to acne and plain, until you bothered to examine her closely, was forever saying wistfully that I had it made. Well, all right, so I did, in the sense that I never had to flaunt my figure or flirt with guys to get their attention. But that was a decidedly mixed blessing. The disadvantage of having long blond hair was that it acted like a candle flame, attracting all the male creepy-crawlies in creation; and their unwelcome presence frightened off the few decent specimens. If the Handsome Hulk were to show up now, I thought, he would take one look at this jerk sitting

7

opposite me, jump to the wrong conclusion, and that would be that!

I swept my hair back and glowered resentfully towards Baldie. He was telling Lynn a joke, but he stopped in mid sentence and smiled at me. I wasn't prepared for the transformation. I forgot my resentment; I forgot that he was bald; I forgot to breathe.

"Go on . . ." Lynn prompted him. "What did he say?"

"Who?" He looked at her blankly.

"Van der Merwe. What did he say to the prostit—" She glanced from his face to mine and back. "Ag, never mind. Forget it. You needn't finish. I think I've heard it before."

"Ya? Probably," he said apologetically. "It's not a very good joke, anyway."

He concentrated on eating the remains of his hot dog. I swung my hair in front of my eyes and studied him covertly through it. I became intrigued by the way his ears jiggled slightly up and down as he chewed.

Munching the last mouthful, he asked, "So what are the two of you doing at this cram college? Taking your Matric?"

Lynn waited to see if I would reply. When I didn't, she said, "You mean we look that young? No, actually Rhond and me took our Matric last year. Not here—in a school. Now we're just killing time, you know, doing a stupid shorthand course. It's bladdy boring, a real drag. And you?"

"Me?" He shifted uncomfortably in his seat. "I'm studying for my Matric."

"No kidding?" Lynn said. "I thought . . . you look older than . . . you mean you're only seventeen?"

"Nineteen."

"Oh. What happened, then? Did you flunk once or twice?"

The instant change in his expression was startling. His face tightened and flushed very dark. "For your information, I started school late. I didn't fail any year, and this is my first go at Matric. Satisfied?"

Lynn appeared to be struck dumb. He sat forward and contemplated her. A faint half smile dented the corners of his mouth.

"Did you know," he said, "that your mascara has run?"

"Really? Which eye?" She dived for her bag on the floor. "Why didn't you tell me, Rhond?" The question was rhetorical; she was already peering in her compact mirror.

From his trouser pocket he pulled out a new packet of cigarettes and peeled off the cellophane wrapping. He had nice hands: broad and supple, with strong knuckles and long, sensitive fingers that dexterously tore a neat hole in the top of the packet. I was too fascinated to realize I was now staring openly at him, until he turned his head. I started guiltily.

His eyes changed color like a chameleon. They were a warm glowing topaz. He didn't smile or speak. Neither did I. I felt peculiarly breathless.

"Shit!" Lynn said suddenly, very loudly. "I've got another chorb coming on my chin."

He laughed. She thrust her compact into her bag and dumped the bag under the table.

9

"It's not bladdy funny," she told him, pouting.

"No, it's not," he agreed. "But you are. You know—I like you." He tilted his chair backwards, grinning at her from under his eyebrows.

"Oh ya? Me and my chorbs and all?" She smirked self-mockingly; her face, though, was glowing.

He went on, "I'll tell you a cure for pimples, the best cure—sex. Seriously, I'm not kidding. It's a fact. Sex once a day; you must have it at least once a day for the cure to be really effective."

Lynn snorted. "I should be so lucky."

"So should we all," he said, and that seemed sufficient cause to set them both laughing. Their amusement jarred on my nerves.

He was trying to catch my eye. I stared coldly past him into space. He picked up his cigarettes and stretched out across the table, holding the packet of Texan right under my nose.

"Smoke?"

Without looking at him or the packet, I said, "No . . . thank you."

He offered Lynn a cigarette, helped himself to one; and then he helped himself to my matches. "D'you mind?"

I shrugged and turned my back to search for the Handsome Hulk. He *definitely* wasn't in the canteen, and he was unlikely to appear now, this late in the day. It occurred to me that he might not be a student at the college, merely a visitor or a friend of a student—in which case, my chances of seeing him again were virtually nil.

Behind me, Lynn and Baldie were exchanging banter. Lynn was giggling. Suddenly, I had had enough. I felt bored, disgruntled, fed up with my life. And the present company was only exacerbating my mood. I swung round and gathered up my things.

"Hey, what you doing?" Lynn demanded.

"I've got to go."

"Go? Where? It's early yet."

"Home. I'll see you tomorrow."

"Rhond!" She grabbed my wrist as I was squeezing past behind her chair. "Why the big rush? What's the matter?"

"Nothing." I tried to shake her off, but she tightened her grip.

"Nothing? . . . You sure? Hey, you're not baddies with me, are you?"

"Of course not," I snapped. "I've just got to get home, I told you."

I was aware of the intense magnetic gaze of green eyes in the background. Lynn was still hanging on to my arm.

"Why?" she insisted.

Some instinct of self-preservation made me lie. "I'm supposed to be meeting Brian at four o'clock."

"You didn't tell me. I thought you never wanted to see him again. That's what you—"

"Well, I changed my mind, Look, I can't stand here nattering. I'm in a hurry. I'll talk to you tomorrow." I wrenched my wrist free and stalked off.

I hadn't gone more than a dozen paces when Baldie caught up to me.

"You forgot something," he said. Taking hold of my hand, he prized the fingers open, placed my box of matches on the palm, and closed my fingers over it.

I snatched my hand away. It was tingling and hot, as if

11

an electric current had sensitized the skin. I stared at him mutely. A group of students brushed past us and one of them bumped his shoulder. He moved aside, then stepped closer to me.

"Uh . . . listen . . . how about—would you like a lift home on my motorbike, as you're in a hurry? It'll be a lot quicker than waiting for the bus."

I hesitated. More students pushed between us, forcing him to move aside again. He was now standing directly under one of the ceiling lights. The rounded dome of his head gleamed unattractively. My earlier feeling of resentment flared up.

"I don't want a lift—thank you. I prefer to catch the bus."

"Okay. Suit yourself." And he turned abruptly and went back the way he had come.

On the escalator, as I was going down to the ground floor, my anger hit me. Who the hell did he think he was, grabbing and hanging on to my hand like that? Didn't he ever bother to look in a mirror? Didn't he *know* how repulsive he was with no hair?

Emerging from the college building, I couldn't avoid noticing the motley assortment of motorized two-wheelers lined up along the railings. I cast my eye down the row, trying to guess which bike would be Baldie's. No doubt it was the awful monstrosity covered with stickers and vulgar slogans, and sporting a multitude of little gaudy colored pennants along the handlebar. Yes, that would be just his style! Not that I cared two hoots, anyway. Much as I might be tempted by the idea of a ride, I would have

12

to have rocks in my head to get on the back of any motorbike belonging to *him*.

My bus stop was only a little distance down the street from the college. I huddled in a nearby doorway to escape the wind that was typical of mid-August, dry and dusty. Shivering, I cursed myself for having decided to wear a short skirt in order to show off my legs to the Handsome Hulk. I was paying for my vanity and high hopes now; my knees were covered in goose pimples and turning an ugly pinkish purple.

A bus finally appeared, but it wasn't the right one. I moved to the curb to see if there was a second bus in the traffic behind it. For some unknown reason, buses often arrived at this stop in pairs—as if they were afraid to travel through the center of Johannesburg on their own.

No other bus was in sight. A small dust devil, swirling past in the gutter, blew grit into my eyes. I rubbed at my eyelids, then jerked my head up at the roar of an approaching motorbike. It was coming towards me rather fast, hugging the curb and overtaking cars hazardously on the left-hand side. The two people astride it were instantly recognizable, even though they were wearing crash helmets. Baldie and Lynn! Lynn noticed me first and signaled Baldie to stop the bike. He looked at me grimly for a long second. Then he swerved out behind a car and accelerated away down the middle of the road.

I took a deep breath. My chest was painfully tight. With the crash helmet concealing his baldness, his appearance was quite different. The difference was stunning! And that look he had given me: angry, defiant, sullen, sensual—

13

my breath caught in my throat. The cast of his features reminded me of somebody, someone famous. But who—?

My bus had arrived. I went upstairs and sat in my usual seat near the front. From habit I took out my shorthand book and opened it at the exercise I had been working on in the lesson that morning. The lines of squiggly symbols began to twitch and squirm up and down on the page. Lynn was right; they did resemble threadworms.

I frowned out the window. Where would the two of them be going? Back to Lynn's house? Or somewhere else? But where else might they go? It would all depend, of course, on what they had in mind. I couldn't be certain of Lynn's intentions, though I was prepared to bet all the money in my savings account on Baldie's. He had to be the sort of guy who picked up girls for one reason only. Why else would he carry two crash helmets around with him? . . . Dammit! I didn't want to think about them. They could go to hell for all I cared.

The book started sliding off my lap as the bus turned a corner. I retrieved it and attempted to concentrate on the first line of squiggles. After a minute, I gave up and shoved the book into my shoulder bag. I wasn't even halfway through the course, and already I was bored to tears. Leaning back, I closed my eyes and conjured up a fantasy involving an older man whom I had met briefly at my father's golf club a few months ago. He was a bigwig in a mining company, and his name was Charles Clarke. That was all I knew about him. But he was tall and tanned, with fine, elegant features and marine-blue eyes, and sleek raven hair turning silvery gray at the temples. His suave manner and charm had enthralled me.

14

. . . We were sitting in his car, which was parked under a tree at Zoo Lake. He had his hand on my knee, and my head rested on his shoulder. We weren't talking—words were unnecessary. The silence between us was charged with a romantic eroticism. I knew the moment before that he was going to kiss me. He did so, very gently and persuasively. The contact of his lips was like the touch of static electricity; my whole body tingled from it. He smiled, and I knew exactly what he was going to say. I was waiting with bated breath for him to say it. He said:

"Ticket?"

I snapped upright. The conductor was leering down at me.

"Ag, I'm sorry, hey, miss," he said. "Did I give youse a scare?"

I fumbled in my purse for the fare. When he handed me my ticket, he touched my hand. The rims of his fingernails were encrusted with black grime.

"Are youse doing anything tonight?"

I turned my shoulder on him. He got the message and shambled off, muttering. I was left seething inwardly. He had spoiled my fantasy. When I attempted to re-create it, Charles's car turned into Brian's Mini Cooper and Charles into Brian, panting as he tried to paw me. "Oh, come on, Rhonda—please! What's wrong? What's the matter with you, for God's sake? You're supposed to like it, you know."

The awful thing was that when I had explained to Brian—as diplomatically as possible—why I didn't appreciate being groped and slobbered over, he had merely been convinced that I *was* abnormal. Worse still, he had ended up almost convincing me as well. After all, it wasn't as if I were

15

sweet sixteen and never been kissed. I was eighteen and had necked with dozens of boyfriends, not one of whom had turned me on. Not one. Of course, I could claim that they were all creeps. But my family hadn't thought they *all* were, nor had my friends. . . .

I became aware that I was tearing little bits out of my ticket. I slid the crumpled remnant under my watch strap and clasped my hands tensely in my lap.

What if Brian was right? What if I was abnormal? The only way to find out was to kiss someone like Charles Clarke or the Handsome Hulk; someone who turned you on just by the way they looked at you. . . . James Dean! . . . James Dean? Yes, of course! *That* was whom Baldie had reminded me of on his motorbike.

The fronds of a palm tree passed by outside the window, and I suddenly realized the bus had reached Rosebank. As I ran down the stairs, the conductor was lolling on the platform. He held out a hand to help me off the bus; I knocked it aside with my elbow and took a flying leap onto the sidewalk.

two

Now that I was almost home, I had little desire to get there in a hurry. I wandered aimlessly around the shopping center for ten minutes or so. Then on a sudden impulse I went into a bookshop and hunted for a book on James Dean. Halfway through the search, I abandoned it and walked out again. Crossing Oxford Road, I set off reluctantly down Tyrwhitt Avenue. The nearer I got to our house, the slower my steps became. Finally, I drew up in a patch of sunlight to have a cigarette. I was scrabbling about in my bag for matches when my young brother, Mark, came pedaling along on his bicycle. He steered it onto the sidewalk and made straight for me. I had to jump back to avoid the front wheel running over my foot, as he applied the brakes at the last possible moment.

"You silly little fool," I hissed.

He was gawking at the unlit cigarette in my mouth. "You're smoking! Oh boy! I caught you smoking. Wait till Mom and Dad hear about it. They'll zap you."

"Don't talk twaddle. I'm old enough to do what I like." I went on looking for my matches.

"So what? Mom'll still zap you. Want to bet?" His eyes remained glued on the cigarette as I pushed it back into the packet. "Hey, don't put 'em away. I'll make a deal. Give me one and I won't tell on you."

"Go and tell. I'm not stopping you."

I walked on, hoping he wouldn't follow me. But of course he did.

"Please, Rhond . . . Pleeeez! Don't be a meanie, Rhond. Pleeeez. Just one, to try. Just one, hey, Rhond?"

I ignored him. He swerved his bike round in front of me, barring the way.

"Pleeeez, Rhond."

"Oh cut it out, Mark, will you—for Pete's sake! You know perfectly damn well that I won't give you a—"

"Why? Why won't you?"

I curbed my temper. Being angry wasn't going to get rid of him; he was in *that* sort of a mood. I said, "Because you're only eight, that's why. You're far too young to smoke."

He gave the pedal his foot was resting on a savage kick that sent both pedals spinning round backwards. "It's bloody not fair. That's what every-bloody-body says about every-bloody-thing I ask for."

"What do you mean? Who's everybody?"

"Just everybody. Bloody everybody." Swinging his leg

18

over the saddle, he mounted the bike and sat with his head bent, his chin pressing into his chest and his narrow shoulders hunched up, hiding his face.

I sensed he was close to tears and said, more sympathetically, "Okay, so it's everybody in general, but *who* in particular, Markie?"

A small choking sound escaped from him. I laid my hand on his shoulder, and then he burst out, in semi-articulate, angry gulps, "H-Helen . . . Helen's told Mom to s-stop . . . stop Dad getting me a pellet gun . . . for my birth . . . day."

"Oh." I took my hand away and delved in my bag for a tissue. I found one too late; he had already wiped his eyes and his nose on the sleeve of his jersey.

"She's a bitch," he croaked, snuffling. "I hate her. She thinks, now she's married, she's God Almighty and can tell us all what to do. I couldn't care less that she's my sister. I hate her."

"No, you don't, Markie, not really. Anyway, when did all this happen—was she here today?"

"She's still here. She's waiting for you to come home." His nose had started running again. I made him blow it in the tissue. "She won't stop me getting a gun," he continued fiercely. "Nobody can stop me. So you tell her that from me."

"Well, I don't know." I pulled my mouth down in comic apology. "I must confess I don't honestly approve of you having a gun, either."

He glared at me balefully through swollen eyelids, but his expression was no longer very convincing. A self-conscious grin was playing tug-of-war with the scowl on his lips. "That's because you're a girl," he scoffed.

"Bosh! It's because guns are destructive. They're for killing, and I can't see any fun in that. Besides, what's so big and brave and manly about squeezing a little trigger?"

"W-h-e-e-w-w! Boy, you know nothing. Let me tell you, if you're stalking terrs in the bush, in really thick bush, man, and suddenly millions of 'em jump out and surround you—boy-oh-boy, you need a heckuva lot of guts then."

He twisted round on the saddle, imitating the noise of automatic rifle fire as he aimed at imaginary adversaries closing in on him from all directions.

"Stop it!" I had to yell to make him hear me. "Just who's been feeding you all this nonsense about terrorists?"

"*Nonsense?* You don't believe me? Okay, ask Alan. He'll tell you. He nearly was zapped by—"

"Who's Alan?"

"Man, you know—Micky's brother." Micky was one of Mark's *choms*, as he called his friends. "Alan's just got back from fighting the Commies on the border. You ask him, he'll tell you what the Commies do to you if they capture you al—"

"I don't want to hear," I cut in.

"It'll make you *cotch*,"* he said with relish. "They skin—"

"Mark! That's enough. Now listen, I'm going home. Are you coming?"

He shrugged, scowling again. "Well, I couldn't care

---

*vomit

what anybody says. *I'll get a gun—so there!"* Swinging the bike round, he pedaled off furiously in the opposite direction.

The click of the latch on the front gate alerted J.R., Mark's eighteen-month-old golden cocker spaniel. I heard him barking, and next moment he appeared at the side of the house and streaked towards me. He tried to take my bag from me as a welcome, then frantically searched for an alternative. Under the pyracantha hedge he found a dead frog and bounded back into the house with it to announce my arrival. Shrieks sounded from the living room. J.R. reappeared and, as I crossed the patio, circled me, wagging his rump and snuffling loudly through his nose to attract attention to his "present."

My mother was standing in the open doorway, brandishing a rolled-up magazine. I glimpsed Helen on the sofa behind her, hugging her knees with her feet lifted up high off the ground.

"That dratted dog's got hold of something filthy and smelly again, so don't let him touch you," my mother warned. "And don't let him in. Quick! Close the door." She slid the glass panel across in the nick of time. J.R. pressed his nose against it, looking lugubrious—a speciality of spaniels.

"Now you've hurt his feelings," I said, and glanced towards Helen. "It's only a dead frog."

Helen pulled a face, shuddering.

"How are you?" I asked.

Her eyes flicked up and down, criticizing what I was wearing. "I'm okay," she said. "Can't complain."

"Good. And Victor?"

"He's fine too. . . . Oh, I forgot to mention, Mom, he's been promoted."

"But that's wonderful," my mother said. "Rhonda, if you want some coffee, you might have to ask Sophie to make a fresh pot. This pot must be cold by now. Feel it and see. . . . Promoted? That really is good news. He's doing jolly well for himself, isn't he? . . . Is it cold, Rhonda?"

"It's all right," I said. "It's drinkable."

"You know," said Helen proudly, "this is his second promotion in less than a year at the bank."

"Bully for him!" I said.

Helen looked at me, and so did my mother. I tasted my coffee, wrinkled up my nose, and placed the cup smartly back on the tray.

"It tastes awful," I complained to my mother. "It's full of grains."

"That reminds me," she said. "Where's Mark? Have you seen him, Rhonda? He's supposed to be doing his homework, but I bet he isn't."

"He's gone off on his bike. He passed me on the way from the bus stop."

"The little blighter. Do you know where he was going?"

"I presume to Micky's house. He was headed in that direction."

"That makes me very angry. He knows he's not allowed to go out without first telling me. He could have an accident, anything could happen, and we wouldn't know where to start searching for him."

"Now do you understand, Mom, what I mean about

22

him being too young and irresponsible to be given a pellet gun?" Helen put in.

"Your father is not *giving* him the gun, Helen." My mother fluttered her eyelashes in annoyance. "The law won't allow Mark to own a gun until he is sixteen. You know that as well as I do. The gun will belong to your father, and he will let Mark use it only under his supervision. The ammunition will be kept locked up in Brad's gun cupboard, safely out of harm's way."

"Even so, I still think Dad's crazy. What's to stop Mark from finding his own ammunition for it?" Helen turned to me. "Don't you agree, Rhonda, that Mark's not old enough to be trusted with any sort of gun?"

My mother sat up straight. "That is a matter for your father to decide," she said.

"Of course," Helen agreed hastily. "Don't get me wrong. I'm all for Mark learning about guns as soon as he's responsible enough. I agree with Dad that it's essential he knows which end of a gun is which before he's called up to do his military service. Boys must learn to shoot. . . . Mind you, the way things are going, I think girls ought to be taught as well. In fact, I think it would be wise for all of us to learn, don't you, Mom? Victor keeps meaning to teach me to use his pistol."

"He should," said my mother. "While he's at it, perhaps he could give me a few lessons with your father's revolver. I really ought to know how it works, considering I've had to sleep with it under Brad's pillow for the past twenty-two years."

"Hasn't Dad ever shown you?" asked Helen, incredulous.

"He did a long time ago. But I've probably forgotten. I very much doubt I could hit anything now."

"What would you be aiming at? . . . Terrorists, I suppose." And I sneered to disguise the cold, creepy feeling of fear that settled on me whenever this word was used in conversation, which it was increasingly.

My mother smiled stiffly. "I hope to goodness it won't ever come to that. But you know, for all your father's certainty that what's happened in Rhodesia can't happen here, there's no escaping the fact that the Black man today is very different from the way he was a few years ago. You notice the difference every time you walk down the street. Africans used to stand aside to let you pass. Not anymore. Now you have to move out of their path."

Irritably I got up and went over to the other side of the room. Helen's voice pursued me:

"The older Africans like Sophie and Zechariah are still okay. You can trust them. It's the young generation of Blacks who are so aggressive and cheeky. They're the ones who are stirring up all the trouble in the townships. But I can't honestly believe that Sophie would cut your throat, even if there was a general uprising and she was ordered to do so by her own people. Do you think she would?"

"Sophie wouldn't; Zechariah I'm not so sure about," said my mother. "He hasn't been working for us very long. He's always respectful to me, and he's certainly useful in the garden; I don't altogether trust him, though. The problem is you can never tell what they're thinking, can you? And these days, you never know who's been recruited by the Communist infiltrators and who hasn't."

24

I stared through the window at the Black man she was talking about. He was spreading compost on the rockery behind the swimming pool, whistling tunelessly. Nothing in his manner or appearance suggested to me that he might be a terrorist. But then, I hadn't the faintest idea what a terrorist was supposed to look like; and I had no intention of remaining in South Africa long enough to find out.

The fearful political situation was not of my making, and it wasn't my concern. I couldn't do anything about it even if I wanted to, which I didn't—I wasn't politically inclined. I just wanted, desperately, to escape from all the frustrating restrictions imposed on my life here and live somewhere more stimulating—like London, where I could be independent and *free*. Free of the stifling atmosphere of my shallow-minded family; free to read any book I might feel like reading; free to see any film or play I might choose to see; free to travel anywhere in the world without feeling ostracized because of my nationality. Most of all, free of the general and growing fear that the future contained an inevitable Armageddon, an all-out war between Black and White—the visions of which were too ghastly to contemplate.

I had left my bag on the coffee table and went to pick it up. Helen was frowning at my mother's dried flower arrangement.

"Mom, supposing Dad were agreeable," she said, "would you consider emigrating?"

"Good heavens, no. I'm much too old to dig up my roots and start again. Besides, where would we go? Your father would never be happy anywhere else. Neither would

25

I, for that matter. No, whatever happens, we'll stay put. Mind you, if I were your age I might think—why? Is that the reason? Have you and Victor been discussing—"

"You must be joking. Victor and me? Mom, we are *South Africans.* This is *our* country. You ought to know me better than that. I'd never dream of leaving."

"More fool you," I spat at her, and I slung my bag over my shoulder and marched from the room.

Before I was out of earshot along the passage, I heard Helen ask, "What *is* the matter with her today?" and my mother answer, "Premenstrual tension, I suspect. It runs in the family. I used to suffer from it at her age. She'll get over it. I did, once I was married and had started a family."

That was all I needed to hear. My mother's diagnosis of my discontent was so way off the mark as to be ludicrous. It proved only how little she understood me. Bursting into my bedroom, I kicked the door shut and collapsed against it.

Just don't let me end up like my mother, or Helen, I told myself.

I felt as if I were choking and stumbled over to the bed. I flopped down on the end of it in front of the window, which Sophie, our African maid, had left wide open to air the room. The cool, fresh draft on my face calmed me. I let my gaze wander over the familiar view of the garden: flower beds in the immediate foreground, then a broad sweep of lawn—the color of a faded yellow duster at this time of the year—hemmed with an embroidery of low-growing ornamental shrubs, then rows of vegetables, a line of fruit trees, finally the perimeter hedge of pyracantha. By craning my neck to the left and right, I could also see part of the tennis court and the swimming pool at opposite ends of the garden.

I love it, I thought. *I have to admit I do love living in a big house with a large garden. But it's not enough, dammit. It's not everything. I would leave South Africa tomorrow— tonight—*right now, *if only I could!*

The awful bind was I knew I had to get some sort of university degree first. A few months working as a filing-clerk-cum-two-fingered-typist in my father's architectural company, followed by this tedious shorthand course at college, had convinced me I didn't want to end up in an office. I had already made up my mind to go to university the following year, which meant I had to stay here for at least another three years. That seemed like a lifetime. *Three* more years of living at home; socializing with the same stupid, boring set of people, listening to the same monotonous family discussions and petty disagreements at the dinner table night after night after night.

"God! I really don't know if I can stand it," I muttered.

I was starting to shiver and closed the window. I resented having to squeeze my hand through the small aperture in the burglarproofing to grasp the catch.

That's another thing—I want to live in a place that doesn't need to have bars over every damn window, I groused to myself as I delved in my bag for my cigarettes and matches. Finding them, I lay back on the bed, stuck a cigarette in my mouth, and opened the matchbox. My finger connected with something inside that was hard and cold and slippery. The unexpectedness of it caused me to drop the box, and the object tumbled out. I eyed it, suspiciously at first, then with curiosity. Finally, dumbfounded, I picked it up and examined it.

It was a small cowrie shell about half an inch long. From above, it resembled a wild bird's egg: oval in outline, smooth, rounded, glistening; palest salmon pink at the edges, darkening to a delicate mauve—the color of a half-healed bruise—on the top. Two elliptical orange lines, which didn't quite meet at either end, enclosed the bruise.

I turned the cowrie over. Its ivory underside was in the shape of a mouth with flattened, slightly open lips, puckered along their inner margins by a row of little perpendicular ridges rather like the teeth of a comb. The narrow opening between the lips suggested a somewhat crooked smile.

I was smiling myself by now. It had only taken me a few seconds to realize how the shell had got into my box of matches. But why? Why had he put it there?

Funny boy! Baldie—Dave. D-a-v-e . . . I repeated the name slowly, experimentally, conjuring up an image of a saturnine face with a James Dean scowl, strikingly handsome in a crash helmet. His green eyes were staring intently at me. Green eyes? Gold-green? Topaz? Amber? Their ardent expression made me feel ridiculously light-headed. I blotted the eyes out with a picture of a bald, gleaming skull, but they came back. Then the whole face reappeared, its sullenness transformed by a sudden irresistible, quicksilver smile.

I closed my mind to the images. *No, I can't, I can't feel that way about him; he's not my type,* I told myself, and I looked down at the cowrie. The hand holding it was trembling, giving the lie to my words.

three

The following day, Friday, Lynn was not at college. Neither was Dave. I sat in the canteen for over an hour, waiting for one or both of them to appear. Then I caught the bus home and rang Lynn. She couldn't talk to me for very long as she was on the point of leaving to spend the weekend on her cousin's yacht at Hartbeespoort Dam.

"I would have told you about it yesterday," she said, "only you shot off in such a hurry. Listen, was Dave there today?"

I feigned surprise. "Dave? How should I know? I didn't see him." An uncontrollable feeling of jealousy sharpened my tone. "I presumed the two of you had decided to take the day off."

"Fat chance! How's it with Brian? Did you—"

"I've decided to get rid of him," I said quickly.

"True's God? Dave will be glad." She laughed. "He really fancies you a lot. I got fed up with all the questions he kept asking me about you, so I gave him your telephone number. I didn't think you'd mind. He's quite something else, you know, Rhond."

"You reckon?" I said guardedly, but she wasn't fooled.

"I knew you wouldn't mind. . . . Well, give him my love when he rings."

"If he rings," I said.

"He will," she assured me.

But he didn't ring me. He didn't ring me that evening, or the next day, Saturday, or on Sunday, either. Not that I sat around waiting for his call—I refused to allow myself to go that far. I went out on Saturday morning and in the afternoon, although I have to admit I did make certain there would be somebody at home to take any messages while I was gone.

In the morning, I visited Wendy, who had been my closest friend all through high school. She was now at university, studying for a degree in fine arts. Unlike me, she had always been clear about what she wanted to do with her life; she wanted to be an artist.

I hadn't seen Wendy for some time. At the end of our last year at school, it had been inconceivable to us both that we could ever drift apart. And yet we had, very quickly it seemed, once the Christmas holidays had ended and the university year began. In the beginning we had tried to keep in contact, but each time we met, we found we had less and less in common; her life on campus and mine behind a desk in my father's office appeared to be worlds apart.

Now, however, having decided to join her world, I wanted to talk to her about university. I think I was also hoping my visit might help to revive our friendship. What a hope! I found her changed beyond all recognition. Her hair was dyed orange and arranged in the Bo Derek style: tight plaits sprouted from all over her scalp and hung down to the shoulders in narrow, stiff tendrils, weighted at the ends by threads of colored beads and imitation jewels that blinded the eye whenever she moved her head. And she was wearing orange eye makeup and lipstick and an orange kaftan and orange sandals.

Her appearance, she explained, was symbolic of the sun. "Like, I'm really into the sun at the moment," she said.

I gathered that she was really into drugs as well, and a boyfriend—a fellow art student, who had apparently introduced her to marijuana and was planning to take her on an LSD trip as soon as he had acquired a fresh supply of the stuff. According to Wendy, her boyfriend was high half the time, which was when, she said, he produced his best paintings.

I asked her to show me some of the work she was doing at university. But she described it all as "a load of crap," and showed me instead a painting she and her boyfriend had done together while under the influence of hash. She called the painting *Black Hole*. It consisted of a spiral, painted in different colors that became darker and darker towards the center; the center was pitch-black. Each color was supposed not only to represent a state of consciousness, but also to have the effect of altering the viewer's own state of consciousness, opening up the "portals of inner vision" until "you're tuned in to a whole new universe, Rhond."

I stared at the black hole. It remained closed to me. I thought the painting and Wendy's interpretation were "a load of crap," but I didn't want to offend her by saying so.

"Very interesting," I muttered.

"Gee, Rhond, you're just not *there*, are you?" she said.

"Nope," I admitted. "I'm not *there*. But then, I'm not high. Maybe that makes the difference."

Wendy laughed.

"Do you ever see anything of Lucie and Rose?" I asked, to change the subject. They were the other two members of our "gang" in our Matric year.

"Lucie and Rose? You mean our two little B.A.s?" she said sarcastically. "You know what B.A. stands for, don't you? *Bachelor Anglers*." She took her painting away and put it on the easel in the corner of her bedroom, then came back to join me on the floor cushion under the window. "They're only at Wits to find husbands—just like all the rest. But you know them, I don't have to tell you."

I was feeling more and more despondent by the minute and becoming irritable. I said, "So you don't see much of them?"

"I avoid them like the plague. They think *I'm* the plague. I'm too way out for them. I'm right off the map as far as they're concerned. And they can't stand Simon."

"Your boyfriend?"

"Simon, ya. He freaks them out because of the way he dresses and behaves. You should have seen Rose's expression the other day in the canteen when Simon was talking about the affair he'd had with an African girl. The girl worked in his father's factory, and Simon used to sneak in to meet her during the lunch hour and they'd have it off behind all the machinery. Fortunately, they were never caught."

As she laughed, the spiky tentacles of her hair quivered and swayed. I looked round the room that had been a second home to me for five years. At least *it* hadn't changed. The familiar objects of furniture provided visual keys to so many adolescent memories.

My eye skimmed over the old display of weathered and torn photographs of male heartthrobs still pinned to the side of the wardrobe next to the bed. At the bottom (where it could be hidden when necessary by Wendy's drawing board) was the male nude centerfold from the copy of *Playgirl* I had smuggled in through customs at Jan Smuts Airport. Flanking it were the two immortals: Elvis and—Jimmy! . . . James Dean, posed on a motorbike, wearing a crash helmet and the famous pout. I had temporarily forgotten that particular photo of him, though it must have been imprinted on the back of my mind all the time. I was about to get up to have a closer look at it when Wendy's voice stopped me.

"Rhond? Jeez, don't tell me *you're* shocked?"

It took me a moment to latch onto her meaning; then I shrugged and mumbled something incoherent.

"You are shocked!" She sneered. "You're as bad as

Rose! For Christ's sake, what's so terrible about Simon having an affair with a Black girl? I suppose you think it's unnatural."

"What if I do?" I snapped, glaring at her. My face was red. "It's none of my business, anyway. And if he wants to risk imprisonment by breaking the Immorality Act, it's his funeral."

"Oh wow! . . . Man-oh-man! You—we're all so bloody hidebound." Leaping up, she stormed off across the room. "Shit! I need a joint right now"—she was rummaging in a drawer—"and I haven't even got some ordinary damn smokes. I must have finished them. Do you have any?"

Churlishly, I threw her a Dunhill and lit one for myself. She borrowed my matches, then lay down on her back on the carpet, resting her bare feet on the cushion beside me. The half-moon of each of her toenails was painted orange (to represent a rising sun, I presumed), with orange rays extending up the nail.

"So what's new with you?" she said. "Jeez, these filter tips taste lousy after grass. But I daren't keep any dope here in case my mother discovers it. She's forever snooping round my room while I'm out. I have to leave anything I don't want her to find at Simon's place. He lives in this old house in Melville, with a lot of other students. It's great. We can do what we like there." She sucked in a lungful of smoke and let it dribble out slowly. "My mother would hit the roof if she knew I was sleeping with him. She only met him once. That was enough. He horr—" A fit of coughing convulsed her.

I observed her coldly for a moment. Then I asked tersely, "Are you all right?"

"Must get . . . s-some water." And she rushed away, spluttering.

When she returned, I was standing in front of the display of photographs, studying them. She came to stand beside me.

"This photo of James Dean—do you still want it?" I asked.

"Do you want it? Take it. Take the lot. I meant to get rid of them ages ago."

"I only want this one," I told her, and I crouched down and, using my key ring as a lever, worked the drawing pins out of the wood.

As I stood up with the photo, she had a smile on her face that clearly said, *Aren't we a little old now for this sort of thing?*

"It reminds me of someone," I muttered.

"Who? Ian?"

"Ian?"

"Isn't his name Ian? The guy you brought to my Easter party. He's an editor or reporter or something."

"You mean Ivor? God, that was months ago."

"Oh wow." She laughed. "Sorry, but it's difficult to keep up with you. Who's it now, then?"

I looked at my watch. "Nobody."

"You've got to go?"

"Yes. I promised to play golf with my father this afternoon, and I need to practice some putts beforehand. I'm terribly rusty."

We parted with obvious mutual relief. Walking out the door, I remembered I hadn't mentioned what had been the main reason for my visit. But I didn't turn back; there seemed no point.

I drove my mother's Peugeot home at reckless speed and found a telephone message waiting for me. It was from Brian. He wanted me to return his call, which I had no intention of doing.

four

My father lowered his glass of whisky and studied me, smiling. We were sitting in a quiet corner of the club lounge, having a drink after our round of golf. My father is big and burly and blond, with dark velvety-brown eyes. When he smiles in the special way he was smiling at me now, his eyes have the warm liquid glow of coffee liqueur.

"Well, Rhonnie," he said.

"Well, Dad." I sensed what was coming. He and I share a strange type of telepathic communication. We have always been acutely sensitive to each other's moods and feelings. To delay him, I said, "I'm sorry I wasn't any competition for you today. I don't know what was wrong with me. Out of practice, I suppose."

He didn't respond. I sipped some sherry and smacked my lips appreciatively.

"It's nice. Not too sweet and not too dry. Just as I like it."

"Good." He took a gulp from his own glass; then he settled back in his chair and cleared his throat. Casually, he said, "Any further thoughts yet, Rhonnie, about what you want to do next year?"

I made a wry face. "I knew you were going to ask me that. I suspected it was the reason you invited me to play golf—to talk about my future. Right?"

"Honey, I invited you to play golf with me because it's the only way I can have you to myself for a few hours these days. Now that you've grown up and all the young bloods in Johannesburg are fighting to take you out, your old dad doesn't get a look in. I have to join the queue and book an appointment, simply to have a chat with you."

"Come off it, Dad. Don't exaggerate."

Normally he could have relied on me to laugh, but his teasing had hit a newly exposed nerve. I looked away, at the two elderly women sitting across the room, talking golf rather loudly over a pot of tea. Then I contemplated the huge painted portrait of Queen Elizabeth II hanging on the wall behind them. Finally I looked back at him.

"I *have* been thinking about my future," I said, "and . . . you were right, I admit it. A degree *is* essential. I realize that now. I'm no clearer as to what sort of job I want to do, but I know one thing: I'd go bonkers if I had to be stuck in an office for the rest of my life."

"Atta girl!" Beaming, he bounced forward in his chair,

grabbed my hand and gave it a tight squeeze, quaffed the remains of his whisky, grabbed my hand again, and glanced about in search of the African wine steward. "Where's that old rascal Jonas? We must celebrate, Rhonnie. You know—you know I can't tell you how pleased I—"

"Dad, there's something—"

"Hang on, here's Jonas. What'll you have? Another sherry?"

"I'm not sure I ought to. It might make me tipsy."

"Ag, what the blazes. We're entitled to get a little tipsy. It's a celebration. You have a sherry. I think I'll have a double." He stood up to pull his wallet from his back pocket; the steward, meanwhile, had collected a few empty glasses and gone out again. "Darn!" my father said. "Missed him. Never mind. I'll nip into the bar and fetch them myself. It'll be quicker. You stay put. I won't be long."

He walked away with a spring in his step. I loved him more than anyone else in the world, and for the moment I had made him happy. That should have made me happy as well. It didn't, because I hadn't finished saying all I wanted to; there was more to come, which, instinct warned me, was not going to go down very well with him. I slumped in my chair, brooding.

After a while, my hand felt into my bag, lying open on the table, and brought out the photo of James Dean. I held it up. Then I realized the two elderly women were staring in my direction, and I slipped the photo back in my bag. Why hadn't he rung me? *Why?* Lynn had been so certain he would.

Glumly, I gazed out the window until my father returned with our drinks.

"Sorry about the delay, honey," he said. "I ran into Charlie—"

"Clarke?"

"Huh? Come again?"

"The man you introduced me to the last time I was here. He's a mining house executive or something. You know, Dad—Charles Clarke." I was careful not to let anything show in my face.

"Oh, *Charles* Clarke. No, this is Charlie Anderson. I don't think you've met him. Little chubby fellow with a ginger mustache; works on the stock exchange. Useful chap to know. He gives me good tips about my shares."

"So you had to buy him a drink to keep in his favor. Honestly, Dad! You businessmen—you're all such hypocrites."

"Hey"—he winced—"give me a break, honey. I didn't buy *him* a drink. He forced one on me when he heard we were celebrating. I had to accept, to stop him coming back with me to meet you."

"Didn't you want him to meet me?"

"Over my dead body."

"Why?"

"Let's just say Charlie is not to be trusted when it comes to attractive young girls under twenty." He looked embarrassed.

"What about Charles Clarke?" I asked, after a pause. "You introduced him to me, so I presume you trust *him*."

"I wouldn't say that. I don't trust any man with you. It's a terrible worry, you know, being the father of a beautiful daughter."

"Dad, stop it. I'm *not* beautiful. Just because I've got

40

blond hair—I wish I didn't have. Blondes are treated as some sort of sex symbol. It's—"

"They are? Then why have I missed out? I'm jealous. I've never been treated—"

"Dad!" I shook my head. "Oh, you're impossible."

Grinning, he reached for his glass and held it up. "To you, Rhonnie, and to your future."

We clinked glasses and drank. He took out a cigar and went through the little ritual of preparing it.

"I think I'll join you," I said.

I found my packet of cigarettes and stuck one in my mouth, steeling myself for his reaction. But he offered me a light without comment. Then he lounged back, puffing on his cigar, and regarded me with mild amusement.

"Does your mother know you've started smoking?"

"I haven't told her, if that's what you mean. I don't see any reason to. I'm old enough to make up my own mind about these things."

"You are, ya." His gaze wandered over me, as if he needed to remind himself of the fact. "Ya, you are. . . . And so, have you made up your own mind yet as to what you want to study at Wits?"

"That's something . . . that's what I wanted to ask— talk to you about. What—what I'd really like to do, Dad, is go to a university in England." I put my glass down, no longer looking at him because I was afraid of what I might find in his expression. His silence was a bad omen. Hurriedly, I said, "Of course, I do realize it would be a lot more expensive."

"You're damn right. It would be a lot more expensive, a helluva lot more expensive."

"But there may be scholarships or grants I could apply for, with my Matric. My four distinctions ought to count for something. I would have thought I stood a—"

"Why, Rhonnie? Tell me why you want to go to university in Britain. What's wrong with Wits?"

I swallowed, watching him relight his cigar. When his face disappeared behind billows of smoke, I said, "You probably won't agree with me, but I feel I would have a much wider choice of courses overseas."

"Poppycock! Honey, you surprise me." With a swipe of his hand, he dispersed the smoke. "That's the sort of uninformed opinion I'd expect from a foreigner, not from someone who's grown up in this country. Wits is a damn fine university with a great tradition. Don't forget I went there myself, and I wouldn't—"

"I'm not forgetting."

"I wouldn't send— What makes you think overseas universities are better? Have you spoken to anyone who's studied overseas?"

"No."

The muscles round his mouth hardened. "I'd like you to go to Wits," he said resolutely.

"All right. . . . Okay, you want me to go to Wits, I'll go to Wits."

My cigarette had been burning away unnoticed in the ashtray. I stubbed it out savagely and took a gulp of sherry; it nearly choked me. *Three more bloody years of boredom, frustration, before I could escape. Three more years . . .* My father's eyes were exploring my face. I bent my head, hiding from him, while I struggled with myself.

"Rhonnie?"

I peered up at him balefully with one eye. He was smiling at me. It was impossible not to respond. I scraped my hair back.

"Dad, what do you honestly think is going to happen here?"

"Here?"

"In South Africa. Do you still feel as optimistic about the future?"

"Of course. Of course I do. This is a great country—sure, we have our problems, but we're making progress with them. We're getting ourselves sorted out. The present chaps in government know what they're doing; they're on the right track. Anyway, let's face it, honey, where aren't there problems? When you look at the mess the whole world is in—hell, all I can say is I reckon we're a lot better off here than anywhere else I can think of." He leaned back, sucking at his cigar. A stream of smoke obscured his face.

In a croaky voice, I said, "I'm afraid I don't agree with you."

His face reappeared; it hadn't lost its smile, though his overall expression failed to reassure me. "You don't?"

"No, and I can't stay here, Dad. I'm sorry. I'll go to Wits because you'd like me to, but I think it's only fair to warn you that I won't be—I *can't* stick around in South Africa after that. As soon as I've graduated, I'm off."

"Off where?"

"To London. I want to live in London, Dad."

He plucked his cigar from his mouth, dropped it in the ashtray, and tossed back his drink—the whole double tot. Then he sprang up with his glass.

43

"I need a refill," he said, and left me.

He was away for only two minutes, according to my watch; to me it seemed much longer. He sat down heavily in his chair and looked at me in a cold, hard manner that I resented.

"Tell me why, Rhonnie, why do you want to get out? Dammit, it's young people like you we need here. We're a developing country and we're not exactly overpopulated. We can't afford to lose our most intelligent and educated White youngsters. If they all start thinking like you do and decide to bugger off, then we *can* forget about the future, then there *won't* be a future worth thinking about. Do you understand what I'm saying?"

"Ya, I understand," I said, "only . . ."

"Only what?"

I was searching for some way of explaining my feelings without upsetting him further. I didn't want us to end up in one of our rare heated arguments—they were too painful.

I said, "The truth is, Dad, I'm just not happy living here. There's so much—there are so many things I find frustrating."

"Such as?"

"The general mentality of people, censorship . . . oh, I don't know—everything, really. Life here is so insular, so shut off from the rest of the world. Let's be honest, this isn't exactly where it's all happening, is it?"

"You reckon?" He arched an eyebrow. "Hell, man, give us a chance. Can't you be a little patient? We've come a long way in the past few years. Censorship has eased considerably; we're even allowed to catch a glimpse of a bare bosom onstage every once in a while now."

"Great!" I said. "Lucky us." And I fumbled for a cigarette.

He relit his cigar without offering me a light. I had to ask him for one. He handed over his lighter and sat glaring at me while I struggled to raise a flame.

"It must need a new flint," I said.

"It doesn't have a flint."

"Really? Well, how—"

"Look here, Rhonnie, if you're so unhappy—if you're critical of the way things are, then why the hell don't you do something about it, instead of just opting out and clearing off?"

"Do something?" At last I had got the lighter to work. I felt as if my lungs were going to explode as I inhaled smoke. "Do something? Me? Do what? What do you expect me to do? I can't change people, the whole of society, I can't change—"

"You can't, no, not by running away—that's for sure. Running away doesn't show much spunk, does it? It's the easy way out. Don't you think it would be more to your credit to stay and work towards achieving the sort of values you believe in, in your own society? Don't you think you owe it to your country to—"

"*My* country?" I couldn't restrain myself any longer. "*My* country?" I slammed the lighter down on the table. "This is *not* my country. I didn't *choose* to be born here, and as far as I'm concerned, I don't owe South Africa a single damn thing. And I'm not remaining here for the

45

rest of my life. No way. You think this is a great country. Well, I don't. It's a cultural backwater. A dead end. A dodo. Quite frankly, I don't give two hoots whether it stays White, or goes Black, Brown, Pink, or Red. I'm not sticking around to find out, or to help preserve a mealie-munching mentality that prevents me seeing the films I want to see, reading the books I want to read, watching the television programs I want to watch. God, I hate this place. I can't wait to leave."

"I see."

That was all he said. He picked up his lighter and examined it carefully. When I hurt him, the hurt always boomeranged back on myself.

I mumbled, "I'm sorry if I—"

"No, I'm sorry. I'm sorry you feel that way about our country." He pocketed the lighter and swigged his whisky, staring past me at the group of golfers who were settling themselves noisily in the recess near the window.

I willed him to look at me. Finally he did, and I rasped, "Dad, you know I don't want to leave *you*. I'll miss you. Terribly."

"But you think you want to live in London, do you? Dammit, man, Rhonnie, don't you realize the mess Britain is in at the moment? How will you live? How will you find a job when there are thousands of young, highly qualified British graduates on the dole? You have to face the facts. Britain's economy is in a critical state. And they also have a serious problem there now with Black people, you know."

"You've spilled some ash on your shirt," I said.

"Besides," he went on, as if I hadn't spoken, "you might get corrupted."

"Corrupted? How do you mean?"

"Ag, you know . . ." He rubbed his nose sheepishly, reminding me of Mark. "Some of our young people—a lot of them—seem to get corrupted when they go overseas. Many of them turn into Communists."

"Oh Dad." I started to laugh. "Can you honestly see me turning into a Communist?"

"No. Well . . ." And then he grinned, looking even more like Mark when he is being teased by a member of the family for being afraid to go to bed in the dark. "I hope not, honey. I hope not."

I reached out and in a clumsy, self-conscious gesture brushed the ash off his shirt. He caught my hand and held it.

"Now what would your old dad do without his Rhonnie, eh? You *can't* leave him. Who would he play golf with? . . . Hey, honey, come on. Smile!" He squeezed my fingers. "That was meant to be a joke. I wasn't being serious. Anyway, let's forget about it right now. You're here for another three years, and a lot can happen in that time. You might change your mind."

"I won't. I won't change my mind, Dad." I pulled my hand free and sat back away from him.

"We'll see. Have you finished your drink? I suppose we ought to be thinking about leaving. I'll be in trouble with your date if I don't get you home in time."

Shaking my hair forward, I said, "What date?"

"Aren't you going out tonight?"

"No."

I gulped down the last mouthful of sherry and stood up. He helped me on with my coat. Then he turned me round to face him.

"Honey, before we go . . ." He was swaying slightly; I grasped hold of his arms to steady him. "Before we go, I—look, I don't mean to pry, but you would tell me, wouldn't you, if some bloke was making you unhappy?"

I reddened. "Nobody is—what makes you think a bloke is making me unhappy?"

"I know you haven't been quite yourself of late, and I was wondering . . ." He tilted forward to gaze closely into my eyes. I could smell the whisky on his breath and, more faintly, the familiar astringent aroma of his after-shave. The aroma evoked a whole host of feelings tied up in the past. My grip on his arms tightened. "You sure, honey?" he asked.

"I'm sure." I squeezed him. "But you're drunk, Dad."

"Nonsense."

"You are. You're tipsy. I'll drive the Porsche. Yes?"

"Ya. You drive your old dad home. I'd like that." He slid his arm round my shoulders. "You will tell me, though, if any chap makes you unhappy? If any chap ever makes you unhappy, I'll knock his block off." And pressing me tightly to his side, he began to steer me in a not altogether straight line towards the door.

five

Sunday passed. That is the best I can say about it. The telephone rang at exactly 9:00 A.M., three minutes past two, half past seven, and twenty to ten. None of the calls were for me.

I spent the morning reading the Sunday newspapers and the afternoon listening to records, smoking at least five cigarettes in the privacy of my bedroom, walking aimlessly about the house, picking a fight with Mark and an argument with my mother. After which I refused dinner, had a cathartic cry in the bath, and went straight to bed in the hope of escaping from myself into sleep.

I was still wide awake when, at twenty to ten, the telephone started ringing. I sat up and switched on the light. Nobody came to fetch me. A few minutes later, I crawled to the end of the bed, opened the window, and shoved the matchbox containing Dave's cowrie out through the burglar bars. Then I lay back in the dark and summoned up the image of Charles Clarke kissing me on the front seat of his car. The Zoo Lake setting failed to work. I tried other settings; I speeded up Charles's passion; nothing worked. I felt cold and dead inside.

Sometime after midnight, I tiptoed stealthily along the passage to my father's study. His medical dictionary listed frigidity. Far from reassuring me, the definition merely confirmed my fears. I crept back to bed and lay stretched out on my stomach, with my head buried under the pillow like an ostrich. The shortage of oxygen helped; I did eventually fall asleep.

In the morning I woke up with a headache, and the only thing that stopped me staying in bed was the thought of spending another day like the last. But I was counting on seeing Lynn at college.

She failed to appear. I left the shorthand lesson just as it was about to start and went to look for her in the canteen, without really expecting to find her. It was more than likely that she had decided to have an extra day at Hartbeespoort Dam. I cursed her absence, as it meant I had to sit at a table on my own in a room full of people who all seemed to know each other. Unlike Lynn, I hadn't become friendly with any of the other students.

I made up my mind to leave as soon as I had finished my coffee. I was only halfway through it when Dave walked in. He was talking to two male students and didn't see me immediately, although I was sitting quite near the door. I was suddenly panic-stricken. My one thought was to flee before he spotted me. Grabbing up my bag, I lunged to my feet. And at that precise moment, he turned round and gazed straight at me. His expression didn't alter. He simply stared, and I stared back, half crouched, immobile over the table. Then I realized how silly I must look, and I slid back down in my chair and opened my bag and pretended to be searching in it.

Without needing to raise my head, I knew he was there, standing right in front of me. I sensed his presence. But he didn't speak, and I was forced to glance up.

"Lost something?" he asked.

"No, nothing important." I started to count the loose change in my purse. My fingers behaved as if they were thumbs.

"Not your matches? I hope you haven't lost that box of matches I borrowed from you last week."

His eyes were even more translucent than I remembered. They were the color of clear seawater in a rock pool. I felt hypnotized. He didn't repeat his question. He just looked at me, and then he pulled out a chair and sat down.

"Smoke?"

"W-hat?" I stammered.

He held out a packet of Texan. My hand moved forward like a robot's, but I couldn't extract a cigarette with my five thumbs.

"Here, let me do it," he said. He also had difficulty; his fingers were shaking. The knowledge made me feel as if he was admitting something, which boosted my confidence. "Have you got a light?" he asked.

I gave him my matchbox. He looked inside it.

51

"It's not in there," I told him. "Listen, why did you—what's it supposed to mean?"

He struck a match and lit my cigarette. I inhaled, and coughed. He laughed.

"Too strong for you?"

"You haven't answered my question."

"What question?"

"The shell you put in my matchbox—what's it supposed to mean?"

He smoked his cigarette, grinning at me. "I'll tell you. Sometime. Hey, where's Lynn? Still rowing round and round Hartbeespoort Dam?"

"*Sailing*, you mean."

"Same difference. Do you like sailing?"

"I prefer motorboats," I said. "They're faster."

"And motorbikes?"

"Motorbikes?"

"Do you like motorbikes? They're fast."

"Yes—no. I don't know. I've never been on one." I was tongue-tied with nervousness at what he was going to say next.

He said, feeling my cup, "Your coffee's gone cold. Do you want some fresh?"

"I . . . yes, I wouldn't mind."

"Okay, let's go." He crushed out my cigarette under his in the ashtray and uncoiled from his chair. "Come on," he said.

"Where?" I asked, on my guard suddenly. Things were moving too quickly for me. I was feeling giddy, as if I had drunk something alcoholic on an empty stomach.

"To Hillbrow for some real coffee. The stuff they serve

52

here tastes like mouthwash. Look, don't worry, nothing will happen to you, I promise." And he smiled.

"All right," I heard myself saying.

His motorbike was a Honda 250. I stood and admired it while he tied his briefcase onto the carrier.

"You keep it in beautiful condition," I told him.

"You should have seen it on Friday. You wouldn't have recognized it. I had an accident on the way to college."

"My God! What happened?"

"I had a little altercation with a large Alsatian. The bike was badly damaged. I had to spend the whole week-end—"

"What about the dog?" I cut in. "Was it—"

"The dog? Oh, the dog survived. I managed to avoid it, and hit the curb instead."

"I'm glad," I said. "I mean I'm glad it wasn't killed."

"Thanks very much. Never mind the ruddy dog. What about me?"

"Well, you obviously weren't hurt . . . were you?"

"No." He handed me one crash helmet and put the other one on. "Only my heart," he said, looking at me from under the visor as he fastened the chin strap. He flung his leg over the seat, kicked the starter, revved the engine, and pushed the bike forward off its stand.

Buckling on my helmet, I followed. My knees felt like jelly; I had to brace myself against the carrier. I could see there was very little room on the seat for a passenger. It would be impossible to sit without touching him.

"What's the problem?" he shouted over his shoulder. "Can't you get up? Do you need some help?"

I shook my head. He switched off the engine.

53

"You're not chicken?"

"Me? You must be joking." And with bravado I scrambled up behind him, leaning back as far as I dared. But I was overcome by panic at the thought of going off alone with him to Hillbrow. "Let's . . . why don't we go straight home—to my house. I'll make us some coffee there."

He shrugged and raised himself off the seat to kick the starter. The engine spluttered, roared, and settled into a vibrating throb that became confused with my own accelerated heartbeat. "Okay, we'll go to your place," he shouted. "But stick your arms round me or you'll fall off."

Once we were in motion, I was able to relax and enjoy the sensation of speed. I had confidence in the way he handled the bike. He gave his total concentration to the road and didn't talk to me at all, except to ask for the necessary directions to my house. When we arrived, he braked abruptly in the gateway, despite the gate being open.

"You needn't leave the bike here," I informed him. "Go up the drive."

"I can't," he said. "There's a snake."

"Snake?" I yanked my legs into the air, even though my feet weren't on the ground to begin with. "Wh-ere?"

He pointed. I peered timidly over his shoulder. The snake was lying stretched across the middle of the driveway. I shuddered as it made a sudden movement. Dave put his mouth to my ear.

"Don't panic; it's not real," he whispered. "It's attached to string."

I peered more closely at the snake. It looked very alive to me, until it slithered forward a few inches and I saw

54

the black thread tied round its head. I opened my mouth to yell at Mark, who was obviously responsible and hiding somewhere nearby, but Dave clamped his hand over my lips.

"Sshh! Keep quiet." He motioned me to get off the bike and lifted it onto its stand. From his briefcase he pulled out a ruler, and began to advance through the gateway on tiptoe, crouching forward and holding the ruler out at arm's length in front of him like a club. After a few paces, he stopped and stared hard at the snake. In a tremulous voice, he called, "I think it's a . . . it's a cobra! Yikes!" And he bounded backwards. There was the sound of a suppressed giggle from behind the gatepost, which Dave pretended not to hear. He inched forward again very cautiously towards the snake. "It's okay; I don't think it's alive. I think it's dead," he announced loudly, whereupon the snake obligingly twitched. Dave let out a yelp, leaped into the air, and landed on his bottom with his arms and legs flailing; and Mark burst from his cover, shrieking gleefully.

"I got you, I got you, oh boy, I *skrikked** you. I *skrikked* you both. You thought it was real. You thought it was real, hey Rhond . . . I got—"

"You," said Dave, lunging at him. Mark struggled to free himself, squirming and squealing, but Dave had a firm hold on him. "Who's he? Your brother?" he asked me.

"I'm afraid so," I admitted.

"What should we do with him?"

---

*frightened

55

"Chuck him in the swimming pool," I said promptly.

"Right." He pinioned the protesting Mark under one arm while he removed his crash helmet and gave it to me. "Hang on to this."

Mark was suddenly quiet and no longer wriggling. With his mouth ajar, he was staring up at Dave.

"You're bald!" he exclaimed.

"*Mark!*"

"Well, he is." He started to giggle as Dave released him. "You look funny," he told him. "What happened to your hair?"

"*Mark!* Will you stop being so—"

"You look funny too," Dave said.

"I don't."

"You look funny to me. You've got frecklepox."

"Frecklepox? What's that?"

"Frecklepox, you know, like chickenpox—those things all over your nose. I hope it isn't catching."

"Man, you're barmy," Mark said, and he brayed, which was his current method of expressing humor. "Hey, can I have a ride on your motorbike?"

"No, you cannot," I said.

"Maybe," Dave told him. "Sometime."

"When? When can—" He whipped round at the sound of a car. "That must be Mom. Quick, I want to give her a *skrik*." He darted to the snake, laid it back in its original position, and hid himself behind the gatepost.

Dave remembered that his bike was blocking the entrance and went to fetch it. Knowing my mother's mortal terror of snakes, I thought I ought to stop Mark from frightening her. But there wasn't time. Dave had barely pushed his bike up the drive when my mother's Peugeot appeared. It halted at the gate and my mother climbed out, looked in the letter box, climbed back in, and drove on over the snake without seeming to notice it. Her attention was riveted on Dave as she parked the car, then walked across to where we were standing next to the Honda.

"Hallo, Mom. This is Dave," I said nervously.

She gave him a tight little smile. "Dave who?" she asked.

"Schwartz," Dave said.

Her smile wavered, but only for a split second. "Schwartz? Really? Our doctor's name is Schwartz. No relation, I presume. It's hardly likely; it isn't that uncommon a name, is it. Rhonda, do you know where Mark is? I want him to . . . Oh, there you are," she said, as Mark came running up with his hands behind his back.

"Hey, Mom, guess what I've got."

"Not now," she said. "I haven't time to guess now, Mark. I want you to find Zechariah and tell him to come and take the groceries out of the boot."

"Look, Mom, *look—*"

"Did you hear what I said? Off you go." She brushed aside his hand without so much as a glance at the object dangling from it. Her attention was back on Dave. Mark stomped away, muttering to himself.

Conversationally, I said, "Dave gave me a lift home from college, Mom."

"Oh, did he?" She ran a disapproving eye over the Honda. "I can't say I'm delighted to know that. I don't like the idea of you riding on motorcycles, Rhonda. They're far too dangerous."

"No, they're not," chipped in Dave. "They're not that dangerous if you know how to handle them." My mother's eyebrows shot up at his tone of voice. He glowered at her. Then he unexpectedly grinned. "I'll prove it to you, if you like. I'll take you for a ride round the block."

His grin was magic; my mother laughed, actually laughed.

"That will be the frosty Friday. However, I'm glad to see you at least have the sense to carry a spare helmet for your passenger. I hope you wore it, Rhonda."

"Yes. Quit fretting, Mom. I *did*."

"All right, then. Well, come inside and have some tea."

As we followed her into the house, I tried to catch Dave's eye. But he didn't look at me. I was convinced he wasn't going to stay long, not after this. He must have been put off for life. And I couldn't even think of anything to say to him to ease the situation. I felt as inadequate and gauche as if I were twelve years old again and bringing home a boy to tea for the very first time.

In the hallway, my mother stopped suddenly. J.R. could be heard whining and scratching at the living room door.

"Drat!" she said. "Now who's locked that blasted dog in again? I've told Sophie *always* to make sure he's not shut up in any of the rooms while we're out. He's so destructive!"

When she opened the door, J.R. went wild with excitement. He leaped up at each of us in turn, then tore round and round the room like a small tornado, scattering objects in his path. Watching him, Dave started to laugh, until he intercepted my mother's look of icy fury as she surveyed the chaos. The carpet was littered with chewed-up bits of the morning newspaper, the stuffing from a disemboweled cushion, a soggy mess of torn tissues. A lamp was overturned, and there was a conspicuous puddle on the parquet near the patio door.

My mother called in Sophie. After a short exchange, humiliating to have to witness, Sophie convinced my mother that Mark was to blame for J.R.'s confinement. So Mark was called in and given a dressing-down, while Sophie resentfully proceeded to clean up the mess, grumbling under her breath in her own language. Mark protested his innocence, answered my mother back rudely, and was ordered off to his room. He stormed out, bawling at the top of his lungs.

While all this was going on, Dave and I remained standing in embarrassed silence, just inside the doorway. But at last normality was restored to the room, Sophie returned to the kitchen, my mother followed to organize the tea, and we were left alone. I sank into the nearest chair. My face was burning.

"Sorry," I mumbled.

"Sorry?" He sat down opposite me on the sofa. "What for?"

"The rumpus . . . my family."

He lit two cigarettes and passed one to me. The gesture was somehow reassuring. I smiled at him. The corners of his mouth lifted in a faint suggestion of amusement.

He said, "Your mother is very beautiful."

"Ya? Ya, I guess she is. Everyone thinks so."

Behind the smoke curling up from his cigarette, his eyes were an incandescent amber, almost the color of a flame. "You know, you look like her," he said.

"I don't. I look more like my father. I've got his blond hair and . . ."

"Go on."

But I had lost track of what I was saying. I couldn't concentrate while he had that expression on his face.

Neither of us heard my mother come in. Her voice startled me.

"Since when did you start smoking, Rhonda?"

"Oh! . . . Oh, ages ago," I said flippantly.

She glanced disapprovingly at Dave, as if she suspected him of introducing me to the habit. "You couldn't have been smoking for ages," she said to me. "I've never seen you with a cigarette before."

"Mom! I've been smoking for *ages*. Now will you please leave off. I can smoke if I want to. It's my life. My choice."

"Doesn't your mother mind you smoking?" she said, turning on Dave.

"Only when I pinch her cigarettes," he said.

I laughed. My mother glared at me. "You'll regret it, my girl. You mark my words. You might think it's clever to smoke now, but when you're older, you'll wish you never started. Like your grandfather. He died such a horrible death. . . . That's right, Sophie, just put the tray down here."

Nobody spoke while my mother unloaded the tea things. Sophie, I noticed, seemed fascinated by Dave. She hardly took her eyes off him until she went back to the kitchen with the empty tray.

I had been hoping my mother would leave us to have tea on our own. But she stayed. She sat down next to

60

Dave and made polite conversation for the first few minutes. Then the questioning began.

"Do you live near here?" she asked him.

"No," he said. "No, I don't."

"You don't?" She held her cup poised in midair.

"I live in the southern suburbs." He cleared his throat. "In Turffontein."

"Really?" The cup tilted; my mother lowered it onto the saucer. Turffontein was definitely on the wrong side of the railway tracks. "That *is* a long way from here."

"Not by bike," he said.

My mother had no answer to that. She offered him another biscuit and discovered there were none left. Without any of us noticing, J.R. had sneaked up and helped himself to them. This created a welcome diversion, after which Sophie came to report some crisis in the kitchen and took my mother away with her. But then Mark arrived, his arms laden with model aircraft.

"Do you *smaak** airplanes?" he asked Dave.

"No, he doesn't," I said swiftly. "Mark, don't be a nuisance now. Please! Haven't you got homework you should be doing?"

He played deaf. "Do you *smaak* airplanes?" he repeated in a tone that it clear that his opinion of Dave would rest on his answer.

"Sure," Dave said, whereupon Mark dumped his models on the sofa and began showing them off, one by one.

I tried again in a sterner voice. "Mark, you *must* have some homework to do."

---

*like

"Nope, I've done it." And he went on explaining how the Spitfires had "zapped" the German planes during the war, providing a noisy demonstration of a dogfight in the air round Dave's head.

"That's enough!" I snapped. "I'm certain Dave isn't *that* interested in airplanes."

"He *is*! . . . Aren't you, Dave?" he demanded.

"Sure," said Dave. He winked at me as Mark rescued one of his models from J.R., who was about to take it apart in his teeth.

"Ah no! Look what he's gone and—It's my favorite plane," Mark wailed. "My best plane and he's gone and graunched the whole bloody wing. Now it's had it. I'll have to throw it away. It's not fair. Bloody dog!"

"Let me have a look," Dave offered.

Mark insisted that it couldn't be fixed; but Dave sent him to fetch glue and, with meticulous care, succeeded in repairing the damage.

"Boy, thanks. You're ace," Mark told him admiringly. "How come you know so much about model aircraft?"

"I don't," Dave said. "But I know about wood and glue."

"How come?"

"Because my dad's a carpenter. That's how come."

"Boy, I wish my dad was," said Mark. "My dad's useless at fixing things. Guess what, though? He's buying me a pellet gun for my birthday."

It was time, I decided, for firm action. I gathered up all his models and thrust them at him. "That's enough from you," I said. "Now buzz off."

Scowling at me, he went, but only as far as the door.

"Hey . . . Dave, do you *smaak* pellet guns?"

"Mark!" I warned him.

He protruded his tongue rudely. "Okay, okay. Man! I'm going!"

As he left, he hooked the door with his shoe and slammed it after him, narrowly missing J.R.'s nose. J.R. started whining; I jumped up to let him out. When I turned back, Dave was standing right behind me.

"I've also got to go," he said. "I've promised to help a mate of mine tune his bike. I was meant to meet him five minutes ago."

"Oh," I said. I couldn't say more without revealing my disappointment.

Tucking his chin in, he stared down at me though narrowed eyelids. "You do look like your mother," he said. "Only there is a difference—the difference between moonlight and sunlight, if you know what I mean."

I shook my head, unable to trust my voice. He moved nearer.

"Moonlight is cold, but at least it doesn't burn you up."

My heart was thumping. "So w-which . . . who's supposed to be the moonlight?"

He leaned forward. "Not you," he said at last, quite gruffly, and he grinned. Then he kissed me. And then he was gone.

I heard his bike accelerate down the drive and roar off into the distance. The noise brought my mother to the living room.

"He's left, has— Why are you leaning against the door? Rhonda, are you all right?"

"No, I mean, yes, I'm fine," I said. "I'm fine. *Absolutely* fine." Wearing a goofy smile, I tottered past her and collapsed on the sofa, stretching out on my back with my feet dangling over the end. "I'm fine."

My mother cast a suspicious glance towards the drinks cabinet, then peered into the empty cups on the coffee table.

"He left very suddenly, didn't he?"

"Hmmm!" I said.

"What a funny boy."

"He is," I agreed happily.

"Why on earth does he shave his head? Has he been ill? There must be a reason for it, but it can't be religious. Very religious Jews grow their hair long. . . . Rhonda?"

I came out of myself reluctantly. "Ill? I don't know. And I don't even know if he is Jewish."

"He must be Jewish, with that name."

She began to collect up the crockery. I raised myself on one elbow and frowned at her.

"Does it matter?"

She bridled at my tone. "No, of course it doesn't matter. Why should it?"

"So long as I don't marry him?"

"Rhonda, if you *must* lie on the sofa, please keep your feet off it. Your shoes are filthy. They'll dirty the cover."

I settled my head back and contemplated the ceiling. "I don't care what he is," I said dreamily, speaking more to myself than to her. "The earth moved; that's all that matters."

She wasn't listening now, anyway. She was exclaiming irritably over some ash she had discovered on the carpet.

"Pick it up, will you, before someone treads it into the pile," she said. "I can't see why smokers have to be so careless. I think it's a dreadful pity you've started. Who do these matches belong to?" She held up the box, and I was on my feet in a flash and sprinting towards the door. "Where are you—"

"I've just remembered I have to find something in the garden."

"Well, I'm sure it can wait. I want you to take these dirty cups out to the kitchen so Sophie can wash them."

"It can't wait," I said. But I went back and let her load me up with crockery.

"Why are you looking at me like that?" she asked. "Has my lipstick smudged?"

"No, it's perfect, Mom. Your makeup is perfect, as always." I surprised myself, and her, by planting an impulsive kiss on her cheek. "You know what Dave said to me? He said, 'Your mother is very beautiful.' "

"He said that?" Her peaches-and-cream complexion flushed rose pink. "He is a funny boy."

"You did like him, though, didn't you?" I wanted her to like him; I wanted the whole family—the whole world— to like him.

"Really, Rhonda! I don't know anything about him. He *seems* a nice enough young lad. I'd find him a lot more presentable if he grew his hair. Now will you please hurry up with those things. Sophie's waiting for them."

Sophie was waiting; not for the crockery, however. She was waiting for me.

"Miss Rhonda!" She grabbed my arm. "Quick! Come!"

65

"Hang on! Where do you want me to put these?"

"Just put them quick-quick here in the sink, Miss Rhonda, and come."

"Come where? What is it, Sophie? I haven't got time at the moment to—"

"Sshh! The madam will be here now-now." With her finger to her lips, she beckoned me into the pantry, closed the door, and said in a conspiratorial stage whisper, "Who's that man?"

"What man?"

"That man who was having tea with the madam . . . the one with the shiny head—no hair."

"Dave?" Tersely, I said, "He's a friend of mine. Why?"

"*Your* friend? You sure? He's not the madam's boyfriend?"

I burst out laughing. "What gave you that idea?"

"He's too old for you, Miss Rhonda, isn't it?" She looked askance at me, a frown furrowing her narrow brown face with ebony grooves.

"Old? He's my age."

"Hawu! But he's got no hair already."

"So what?" I felt myself becoming irritable. "So what if he's got no hair? Anyway, he has got hair. He shaves it off."

"Shame," she said, and that restored my sense of humor.

"Are you satisfied now?" I asked. "Can I go?"

She bobbed her head, smiling. "I was so worried, Miss Rhonda. I was praying, praying, praying all the time that the madam wouldn't take the apple from the serpent. I thought maybe there is big-big trouble coming in this house."

66

"There will be big-big trouble if the madam discovers you thought he was her boyfriend," I said, and I left her laughing, and went to search for my shell.

I found it, after trampling on a few of my mother's special selection of bicolor daffodils, grown as a border under my bedroom window. Like a bad penny, Mark turned up as I was trying to revive them.

"What you doing there? Hey, did you zap those flowers? You'll be in for it. Oh boy!" And he flicked his fingers in imitation of a whip.

"You reckon?"

"I know it. You'll be told off, and it'll serve you right for being so soppy. I saw you. Kissing! . . . Urgghh!"

"You little rat! You were spying!"

I took a step towards him. He danced back out of reach, clutching his throat and making retching noises as if he were going to be sick.

"Kissing! . . . Urgghh! . . . Sis on you! . . . Urgghh!"

I walked away without allowing him to see I was grinning. He followed.

"You not cross with me?"

"No. Sorry to disappoint you," I said.

"Boy-oh-boy, you must be in love."

I stopped. "And what makes you think I'm in love, smarty-pants?"

"People act loony when they're in love. They go barmy. Ya, you look barmy to me. True's bob. You must be barmy if you're in love with a *kaalkop*.* Why's he got no hair?"

---

*barehead

"Now I *am* cross," I said. "I'm bloody tired of being asked that. For the *last* time, I *don't know!*"

"Okay, keep your hair on—hey, wait for me. . . . Did you get that? Keep your hair on? It's funny."

"Hilarious!"

"Maybe I should cut all my hair off. I won't have to worry about washing it, then."

"Good idea. Mom'll be charmed."

"Ya." He snickered. "She'll throw a fit, won't she."

I tried the patio door. It was unlocked. I slid it open and Mark wriggled through with me.

"But even if he is a *kaalkop*, he's quite a nice guy," he conceded. "I *smaak* him. He's not such a twerp as all the others."

"All what others?"

"All the other guys you've been out with—Brian and them."

"For once, Markie, I'm in total agree—"

"Crikey! Here comes Mom. Don't tell her you've seen me. I haven't done my homework." Like greased lightning, he streaked across the patio and vanished down the garden.

That night, I must confess, I did something that would probably justify Mark's opinion of my state of mind: I slept with Dave's shell under my pillow.

six

My alarm failed to wake me. I overslept. By the time I arrived at college, the shorthand lesson had ended.

Both Dave and Lynn were in the canteen. They were among a group of students at one of the few large tables, but they weren't sitting together. Dave was seated between the two friends I had seen him with before, at the opposite end of the group from Lynn. He had his back to me and appeared to be engrossed in a conversation.

The chair next to Lynn was empty; with butterflies in my stomach, I walked over and sat down on it. All the way into town, I had been on tenterhooks in anticipation of how Dave would react when he saw me. Now I was afraid to look in his direction. I asked Lynn about her weekend.

"It was nothing special," she said offhandedly. She seemed unusually subdued. "But I've decided to chuck shorthand. It's a bladdy waste of time."

"What'll you do instead?"

"I don't know. Get a job, I suppose, until university starts."

"What sort of job?"

"I don't know. I know what I'd *like* to do—I'd like to go to Israel for a few months, but I doubt my pa will cough up the money."

A girl across the table leaned forward. "Israel? Did you say Israel, Lynn? You should go and work on a kibbutz, like my sister." She began telling Lynn all about her sister.

I sneaked a glance round at Dave and caught him looking at me. The instant our eyes met, his slid away. Confused and hurt, I shrank back in my chair.

A burst of raucous laughter broke out from the students on Lynn's left. They were swapping jokes. Lynn was still talking to the girl opposite. I was trying to decide whether to leave when I became aware that an argument had started at Dave's end of the table. Curbing the impulse to look round, I strained my ears to listen. A male voice, not Dave's, was speaking.

". . . that's crap, Tony. Angola isn't my effing country. Why should I go and get myself carved up fighting Commies in Angola?"

"So who said you'd be sent to—"

"Christ! Where do you think, Tony, all these guys on National Service are spending their time? On some effing parade—"

"They're helping to defend our borders. That's what

they're effing doing. They're stopping the Commies coming in and taking over our country. Your effing country too, Paul. Somebody's got to do it."

"Not me, mate. It's not my fight. Nobody's going to shove me in uniform and send me off to chase Black gooks around the bundu in South-West Africa, or across the border into effing Angola. I don't give a hell what happens in South-West Africa. It's not my effing fight, man."

"That's what you think! I guess you'll be saying, 'It's not my effing fight, man,' when the coons try to take over here too?"

"Don't be bloody stupid. If the coons in this country try to take over, then we'll *all* have to fight, to save our effing skins. I'll have to fight then—if I'm still here. But right now, I've better things to do with my life than spend two years in the effing army. You go off and be a hero, Tony, only when you get yourself shot to pieces, don't expect Dave and me to come looking for bits of you to bring home to bury. Not so, Dave?"

I heard no answer from Dave.

Tony's voice said jeeringly, "You're all mouth, Paul. You're full of crap. Okay, so tell me how you're going to avoid doing your National Service."

"I'll avoid it. I know guys who've managed to. I'll disappear—skip the country, if I have to. . . . Hey, Dave, that's what we should do—take off on our bikes up Africa. Hey, man, what an effing good idea."

I listened for Dave's response. There wasn't one. Tony's scoffing voice started up again. I peered round through my hair. Dave was slouched in his chair, chin sunk on

71

chest, eyes downcast. A heavy brooding frown corrugated his forehead. He had the abstracted and tortured expression of someone immersed in a private mental conflict or torment. Puzzled, I went on observing him, until he glanced up suddenly and I saw what was in his eyes: loathing, contempt—and even more incomprehensible, fear. He wasn't looking at me; his glance was directed at his arguing friends, but the force of his feeling unnerved me.

I thrust my chair back and interrupted Lynn's conversation to tell her I was leaving.

"But you haven't had any coffee yet," she said. I noticed her eyes flick in Dave's direction. "And I haven't asked—Listen, did Dave—"

I cut her off. "It's too noisy in here to talk. Give me a ring sometime."

"Oh, ya . . . sure. 'Bye, Rhond."

" 'Bye." I squeezed her shoulder. "Take care."

She smiled up at me bleakly. "Ya . . . you too."

I made a long detour round tables to avoid walking past Dave. I could feel a headache building up and went into the loo to swallow a painkiller. And that must have been when he managed to slip out of the building ahead of me. As I stepped from the entrance into the blaze of sunlight, there he was—sitting astride his motorbike right in front of me, with the visor of his crash helmet pulled low over his eyes and a cigarette dangling from the corner of his lips. Against the glare, he looked like a shimmering mirage, a hallucinatory image of the photograph of James Dean.

I stood rooted to the spot, blinking.

He removed the cigarette from his mouth and grinned.

That disarming grin of his! It was all it took to sweep away my defenses.

"I want to talk to you," he said. "It's important. I'll give you a lift home." He shot out his hand, and before I had time to collect myself, he had dragged me up on the bike, clamped a helmet on my head, buckled the strap, kicked the starter; and we were speeding off down the street, dodging in and out of the line of cars.

I told him to pull up at our front gate, and I dismounted to see if my mother's car was in the driveway. It was.

"Another snake?" he asked.

"No. My mother's home, so if you want to talk, I think we'd better go somewhere else."

"Where?"

"We could go to the bird sanctuary. It's just down the road. The Melrose Bird Sanctuary. Do you know it? It's beautiful."

"All right, let's go there, then."

We left the bike in the parking area and walked through the gate. I walked ahead of him along the grass. At the first break in the thick belt of reeds bordering the dam, I clambered down the bank to the edge of the water. A few ducks were paddling around pompously in the shallows. I turned to point them out to him. He was standing at the top of the incline with his hands in his pockets, staring down at me very intently.

My mouth dried up. Forgetting what I was going to say concerning the ducks, I scrambled back up the bank past him and onto the grass. He walked towards me. I glanced about. There was nobody within sight. We were alone, completely alone. I backed off a step.

73

"W-what d-did you want to say to me?" I stuttered.

"Were you avoiding me today?"

"M-me? Avoiding you? That's a cheek. You cut me dead."

"Did I? . . . Ya, I did," he admitted. "I know." He grinned briefly. "I'm sorry."

"But w-why . . . why did—"

"I was running away," he said in a thick voice. "I was scared."

I gave a strained laugh. "Of me?"

"Of . . . oh Christ! This is ridiculous. See what I mean?" He held up his hand to show me it was shaking. Then he stretched out and touched my face. His fingers stroked the hair off my eyes. "Crazy." He gulped. His other arm encircled me, and he pulled me close against him.

I clutched him round the waist and we clung together, trembling.

"Crazy . . ." He grasped my chin, and tilted my face up, and kissed me. It was a chaste kiss, little more than a momentary contact of lips. But it awakened something in me, something startlingly new—a deep-centered flicker of desire.

Wide-eyed and breathless, I gazed up at him. He was playing with my hair, caressing it, combing his fingers gently through it.

"It's the exact color of the veld in midsummer," he said. "Palomino gold."

I smiled into his eyes. "So tell me, what were you scared of?"

"Of becoming too involved with you."

I linked my hands more securely behind his waist. "And now?" I asked.

"Now?" His voice had a husky quiver. I could feel his heart hammering.

"Are you still afraid of becoming too involved with me?"

"Ya. . . . No!" And with sudden force, he grasped my face between his palms and pressed his mouth hard on mine. "No . . ." He shuddered. "Christ! No."

I clasped him tighter, returning his kiss hungrily. My mouth welcomed his tongue. Then I panicked and fought to free myself.

"You shouldn't have done that," I gasped. Without giving him time to reply, I walked away from him and perched on a log farther along the bank.

It had happened too fast, too soon. It had suddenly got out of control. I didn't want it to be like this. I wanted it to happen, yes, but not like this. Not before I was sure he . . . oh God, it had to be more than just sex. Please, it *had* to be!

I stiffened as I heard him behind me, striking a match. He walked past to the other end of the log and sat down and smoked his cigarette, staring straight ahead.

"You're right," he said gruffly.

I pulled my hair over my face. "I'm right? . . . Right about what?"

"We should just be friends."

"I didn't—did I say that?"

"I'm saying it. No hassle. No hard feelings. We'll just be friends. Okay?" He stood up and ground his cigarette out under his heel. "How far can you get round the dam?"

"About halfway," I mumbled.

"Would you like to— Hey, look at that black-and-white bird. What is it?"

"It's a pied kingfisher," I told him.

He watched it for a moment. Then he unexpectedly bent double, put his palms on the ground, kicked his feet into the air, and began to walk forward on his hands.

"Come on," he called. "I'll race you."

"No, I can't do that," I said.

"You can. It's easy. I'll show you. Come on."

"I've tried. I can't. Anyway, I've got a headache." The effect of the painkiller was wearing off.

He walked in a circle, keeping a perfect balance, back curved, legs straight and vertical. I feasted my eyes on his body. The front of his shirt had slipped out of his trousers, exposing his midriff. His torso was a lovely honey color and corded with tight muscle. I looked away.

"If you don't mind, I think I ought to go home now," I said, and started towards the entrance.

At the gate, I waited for him. He came up to me, tucking his shirt in and grinning in a self-satisfied manner. It seemed that one of us, at least, was happy at having settled the question of our relationship.

"When I was a kid, I used to make money doing gymnastic tricks," he informed me.

"Where?"

He was suddenly embarrassed. "Ag, I really can't remember," he said. "It was too long ago."

He stopped the bike in front of our house to let me off. I thanked him for the lift and was expecting him to depart

76

immediately. But he sat there, contemplating me, as if he was waiting for something.

I said, "I'd ask you in for a coffee, only I'm going out a little later and I have to wash my hair."

"Who with?"

I was surprised by his aggressive tone. He scowled at me.

"It's a family do," I explained. "Nothing exciting. My brother-in-law is taking us all out to dinner to celebrate his recent promotion."

"Your brother-in-law? That's okay, then." He grinned and released the clutch. The bike plunged forward. A little way down the street, he turned and came back. As he drew level, he shouted, "See you tomorrow. In the canteen." Then he accelerated and disappeared round the corner, leaving me in a state of total confusion.

seven

And so we were friends, supposedly. We met in the canteen each day and left together to have coffee somewhere. But we didn't touch each other, except when we were on the bike and it was unavoidable. Being friends meant *no touching allowed*; Dave's manner made that crystal clear. He kept his distance from me, and whenever I came too close, he instantly moved away.

One compensation was that we talked a lot, and I got to know him better. He wasn't very forthcoming about himself, but I did manage to discover that he was an only child, that his parents were elderly and not well off, and that his feelings for them ran deep. There was an emotional undercurrent in his tone when he spoke of them,

78

which prompted me to remark that they must be quite special and I would like to meet them.

"They're great. I owe them a lot," he said, and abruptly changed the subject.

The following day I found out that he wanted to be a mechanical engineer and intended taking his degree at Wits.

"We'll be there at the same time then," I said.

But he appeared to be less pleased than I was at the prospect, and it was one of many moments when I felt hurt. I just didn't know where I stood with him. I would catch him looking at me in a way that set my pulse racing. Then almost immediately afterwards, he would do or say something to make me feel rebuffed.

It was worse, however, when I wasn't with him. I couldn't settle to anything. I couldn't concentrate on a book, or on music, or on any of my other escape activities. I drifted about in a daydream, holding endless postmortems of our conversations, while his face imposed itself on whatever I was looking at. I couldn't get him out of my mind. I was miserable, and the time between our meetings seemed interminable.

Fortunately, our so-called friendship lasted only three days. At the very last minute on Friday, after Dave had dropped me at the gate and was about to depart, he suddenly asked me if I was free that evening.

"Why?" I said eagerly.

"I'm not doing anything. . . . I don't know. . . . I thought maybe we could go to a film or something. But it's not important. Forget it. I'll see you on—"

79

"Wait!" Impulsively, I grabbed his wrist. His fingers slid off the clutch and the bike stalled. "I'm sorry," I said as he restarted the engine. "I didn't mean to do that, only I'd like to go to a film tonight, if you would."

"Right," he said tersely. "I'll pick you up at about eight." And he took off at top speed.

The evening didn't start well. I was ready half an hour early; Dave arrived late, too late to get to Hillbrow, where the film I wanted to see was showing. We ended up at the local cinema and sat through a slapstick American comedy. It wasn't at all funny, but we laughed loudly in all the right places. Neither of us was relaxed. The seats were uncomfortably close together, and every time Dave shifted position, I tensed; I was conscious of a similar response in him whenever I moved. The end of the film came as a relief.

Out in the street, Dave suggested going for a drink.

"A coffee?" I asked.

"Is that what you'd like?"

"I don't mind. I'm easy."

We were standing on the sidewalk under a streetlamp. In the diffuse glow of light from above, his face was shadowy, incorporeal. He muttered a few words indistinctly. I thought he said, "God, you're beautiful."

"Pardon?" I asked stupidly.

"Skip it. What would you like to do?"

"I really don't mind. What would *you* like to do?"

He let out a hoarse laugh. "You slay me, you know that? Come on, I'd better take you home."

In stiff-lipped silence, I walked beside him to the bike. He talked nonstop. He was trying to be amusing, trying to make me laugh. He didn't succeed. We rode home. He parked the bike in the gateway and insisted on accompanying me up the drive. He was still acting the funnyman. At the door, he snatched my key and put on a Laurel and Hardy performance of clumsy ineptness at finding the keyhole.

The door clicked open; as I stepped forward, it clicked closed, and Dave suddenly grabbed me.

"I'm sorry, but I can't help myself," he said, and he bent his head, gave me a quick peck on the cheek, and ran.

"Dave!" He was halfway down the drive. I kicked off my shoes and tore after him. "Dave, wait!"

He stopped and turned. Just before I reached him, he held out his arms. If he hadn't made that gesture, I've no idea what I would have done or said when I got to him. But as it happened, there was no need to say anything.

"We're mad," he gasped when at last we came up for air. "But I love you."

"Say it again."

"We're mad."

"No, not that."

"Rhonda . . . Oh hell . . ." His arms pulled me in tighter against him.

I nestled my nose into his leather jacket. "Dave—Dave, I think I love you."

"*Think?*" His laugh had a phlegmatic quality I recognized. It was his hurt laugh. "You *think* you love me?" He walked the fingertips of one hand across my cheek, then lifted the hair off my face. "What am I going to do with you?"

"With me?" I tilted my chin up, trying to read his expression in the darkness.

"God, this shouldn't have happened, you know."

"Tonight?"

"Us. We shouldn't have met. It's a mistake. It can't come to any good."

"Why?" I squeezed the word out through the heavy dread blocking my throat. He wouldn't withdraw from me again? Not now? Oh please, not now; not after we had come this far. It would be too cruel.

He closed his eyes and shook his head, as if he was attempting to shake off his own fear or doubt. "I don't know. I just don't see how it'll work out." His fingers were digging into my shoulders. I grasped his hands, and he opened his eyes. The sudden whiteness of his smile reassured me. "It's too late now, anyway. There's nothing I can do about it," he said.

"About? Dave, what—"

"I love you," he said simply.

"I love *you*," I said with complete conviction.

"You do? No more 'think'? What happened to 'think'?" His laugh this time was free, happy. I adored his laugh, all his laughs, *all* of him.

"Think," I said, "died very suddenly of natural causes."

"What natural cause? This? . . . Or this?" He kissed my mouth, my nose. "Or this?" He nuzzled my ear. His tongue began to explore its inner shape. I was overtaken by the powerful erotic effect on other parts of my body. It was something of a shock to discover that my ear was an erogenous zone, because it wasn't exactly virginal. I pushed him away weakly. "Sorry, is it too ticklish?" he asked. "Don't you like it?"

"Too much . . . I . . . think you'd better go." He pretended to take me at my word. I caught his sleeve and yanked him back. "Hey, not so fast."

"If I don't go fast, I won't go."

"You!" I said, biffing him softly under the chin with my fist. "I can't trust you. How am I to be sure you won't just disappear and never come back?"

"I'm coming back. I'm only going to ride round the block to give you a chance to cool off."

"No, be serious. This is serious. When will I see you again, Dave?"

"Tomorrow? . . . Heck, I forgot—Saturdays are out. I work all day, repairing motorcycles. It's a way of making some money. And tomorrow evening, I've promised to help my dad deliver a few cabinets he's made. So it will have to be Sunday. Sunday morning, early. Yes?"

"How early?"

"Six, seven? No, I'm kidding. I can last a little longer than that. Say, ten. Okay?"

"Ten is fine. You promise you'll turn up . . . on time?"

"I'll be there. On the dot. If you aren't out of bed, and I can slip past your mother, I'll come and wake you with a cup of coffee and a kiss."

"I'd like that."

"So would I! . . . Listen, have you still got that shell?"

"I have. Tell me what it means."

"Not now. Keep it safe, though. It's irreplaceable."

"Why won't you—"

"I can't. I can't tell you," he said mysteriously.

"Why not?"

"I'll have to show you."

"When?"

"Sunday. I'll show you on Sunday," he promised, and kissed me. Then he left me in his usual sudden fashion.

eight

Helen looked at Dave as if he were one of J.R.'s presents: not immediately recognizable, but bound to turn out to be rotten on closer investigation. My mother smiled her polite smile. Victor pompously shook Dave's hand. My father greeted him jovially, pulled up a chair for him at the patio table, and offered him a cold beer from the ice bucket. Victor drew up a chair for me. My mother offered me a cup of tea.

"I'd prefer a shandy," I decided.

"Wouldn't you rather have tea? It's better for you," she said pointedly.

"No! I'd like a shandy," I told her.

"Fix the girl a shandy, will you, Victor," said my father.

"I can do it," I said, but Victor had already raised his considerable bulk out of his seat.

"Where's the lemonade?" he asked my father.

"At the bottom of the fridge, in the kitchen. Oh, and while you're at it, fill me up again, will you, there's a good chap."

"Brad!" my mother said. "Do you think you ought—"

"Make it a double, Vic," my father called after his son-in-law. Then he winked at Dave.

My mother quickly said, "Isn't it a heavenly day? It's the nicest day of spring so far. I should have got Sophie to set the table out here. Will the two of you be staying to lunch, Rhonda? I need to—"

"Of course they're staying to lunch," my father cut in.

My mother smiled uncertainly at Dave. "I'm afraid we're having roast pork. But we could cook something else for you. It won't be any trouble."

"How do you know he doesn't like roast pork?" my father asked her.

"Dad!" said Helen. "Some people can't eat pork, Dad, because it's against their religion."

"Against whose religion? Who are you talking about?" Victor asked behind me.

Nobody answered him. He handed my father and me our drinks. I wanted to crawl under the table. Dave was fishing a small insect out of his glass. He cleared his throat.

"Actually, I like pork," he said.

"Oh. Oh, that's a shame," said Helen. "It must be awful to like food you aren't supposed to eat. One of the Jewish teachers at my school is just the same. She loves bacon and—"

"Actually, I'm not Jewish," Dave interrupted her.

"Oh, I see. I'm sorry, I thought you were."

Her face turned red. A look passed between her and my mother, confirming my suspicion that my mother had talked to her about Dave. My father rubbed his nose, covering his mouth to hide his amusement.

"Well"—my mother rose swiftly—"if you'll excuse me, I'll go and see how the dinner is progressing. You must all be hungry. We won't wait for Mark." She swept into the house.

"Where has Mark gone, Dad?" Helen asked.

"He's taken J.R. for a walk, or J.R. has taken him for a walk. They've probably ended up at Micky's house. That's where Mark seems to spend most of his time these days. I suspect Micky's pellet gun is the main attraction."

Helen started to speak, thought better of it, and picked up the woolen romper suit she was knitting for a friend's baby. She consulted the pattern.

Victor heaved himself upright. "Man, it's hot. I'm sweating like a Black," he said in a humorously apologetic tone.

He dabbed at his receding hairline with the monogrammed handkerchief he always carried neatly folded in his breast pocket. Dave watched him. I noticed that my father, who had settled back with his whisky, was scrutinizing Dave out of the corner of his eye.

"Dad, do you reckon this weather means we're in for a good summer?" asked Victor.

My father grunted and took a swig from his glass. He was looking at me now. His faintly quizzical, bemused smile gave me a moment of uneasiness before he spoke.

"So tell us, Rhonnie, where the pair of you have been gallivanting to this morning."

"Nowhere," I said. "We only went for a walk."

"You as well. By golly, what's got into this family? The neighbors must think the Bradleys are turning into fresh air and fitness freaks. How far did you walk?"

"Not far . . . We went to the bird sanctuary." I shook my hair forward as I felt myself blushing.

"The bird sanctuary? Aahh!" said my father. "Did you hear that, Vic? These two went bird-watching this morning."

"Aahh!" said Victor. "Bird-watching, eh? So that's what they call it these days."

"Did you see many birds, Dave?" my father asked.

Victor snickered. Dave's face was dark with embarrassment. But he looked my father straight in the eye.

"Birds?" he said. "What birds?"

My father laughed. We all laughed, except Helen. She managed a constrained smile. Then my mother called out that lunch was ready.

During the meal, my mother and Helen kept the conversation going, mainly by chatting to each other. Victor chipped in from time to time. I sat on the edge of my seat, pushing the food around on my plate and swallowing with difficulty. I tried to think of things to say to Dave, but whenever I opened my mouth to speak, I became aware of my father's pensively watchful gaze trained on us both, and dried up. My mother, at the end of the meal, instructed Sophie to serve the coffee on the patio, and asked me to supervise it.

In the kitchen, while we were waiting for the water to

boil, Sophie said, "That man, Miss Rhonda, you sure-sure he's your boyfriend?"

"Oh, Sophie, come on, now. You could see for your-self—he's not old."

"No, he's not too old. But why's he got no—"

"I've already told you, for heaven's sake! *I don't know.*"

I had forgotten to keep my voice down. A little late, I went and closed the door into the passage.

"Miss Rhonda, maybe . . . you think he's sick?"

"Sick? Rubbish. Does he look sick to you?"

"I can't say, only sometime when people get sick, in the hospital they cut off all their hair."

"Of course he's not sick."

The kettle whistled. Sophie filled the coffeepot and carried it over to the tray. From the back, with her bony elbows sticking out and her thin legs protruding from underneath the green smock, she did resemble a praying mantis, which was what my father called her in jest because of her fundamentalist faith in the Bible.

"Are you going to church this afternoon, Sophie?"

"Always, always, Miss Rhonda, on Sunday I go to church. You know that."

"Yes."

"The Lord Jesus said—"

"Yes, I know. I know what he said," I hastily interrupted her. If you allowed Sophie to start telling you what the Lord Jesus said, she was unstoppable. I inspected the tray. "Where's the cream?"

"It's here. Where's your eyes? See? Here."

"Oh, ya, I'm sorry. I'm blind."

"You know what's the trouble? I think you must be in

89

love, Miss Rhonda. Because when you in love, you can't see anything. It puts out your eyes."

"I am," I said immediately, finding relief in being able to admit it to somebody. "I am in love."

"With that one?" She jerked her head towards the door.

"With him, yes."

She clucked her tongue. "Shame."

"Why shame?" I said, offended. "Look, he doesn't need to have hair, dammit. He's handsome without it. I think he's terrific."

"Maybe. Maybe not. I can't say. But in the Bible, you know what has happened to Samson? His hair was all cut off, all finished, no more hair . . ." Her hands clapped together, then the palms opened outwards. "And *the Lord was departed from him.*—Judges sixteen, Miss Rhonda." She looked at me sideways, with a hint of humor twitching the leathery crevices in her cheek. She had the weather-beaten, wrinkled face of an old woman, although she was only in her forties. "But if your heart is very happy to have him, Miss Rhonda, my heart must be glad for you. I will pray—"

The door had opened. "What's this?" my father said. "A prayer meeting? Where's the coffee, Sophie? Man, we're all dying of thirst out there."

Sophie grabbed up the tray. "The coffee's ready, master. It's coming now-now."

"So's Christmas," he told her laconically, and stood aside to let her pass. "Run, run, *mafutha.**

"*Mafutha*? Me?" She cackled. "No, master. I'm too old

---

*fatty

to run anymore, but not too fat. I'm too thin like a locust. But the master, I think, maybe, is getting more *mafutha* now," she added, grimacing slyly at him over her shoulder as she moved away.

"You're right, Sophie. I'm growing fat and old and gray from worry about my children," he called after her. Then he closed the door and turned to look at me. He appraised me silently.

"I'd better go and join the others," I said. "Dave must be wondering where I've got to. . . . Excuse me, Dad." He was in the way; I couldn't reach the door handle.

"Rhonnie . . ." He chucked me under the chin. "My little girl."

It wasn't the words; it was the self-mocking emphasis he gave them that distressed me. "Dad—"

"I know, I know," he said. "You're a big girl now." He walked past me to the table. "I'm looking for my damn bottle of whisky. Do you think your mother has hidden it?"

"Dad? . . ."

He came back to where I stood, hesitating, with my hand on the door.

"Dad—I hope you like him."

"Dave?"

"Yes. Do you?"

His eyes smiled at me. "I'd like to know why he chooses to go around looking like a bare backside. Have you asked him?"

"I can't. He's a bit sensitive about it."

"Hell, honey, you're in love with the guy and you can't—"

"Am I?" I said, reddening. "How do you know?"

He lifted the hair off my eyes. He and Dave were the only two people who could do that without my minding. "Aren't you?"

"I think so. No! I am, yes," I admitted. "I am in love with him. Don't ask me how or why. It just happened."

He chuckled. "I guess it just does, honey."

Reacting to the slight roughness in his voice, I said defensively, "But he is special. He's sensitive and introspective and interesting and considerate and . . . and he's lovely. He's . . . You don't dislike him, do you, Dad?" I asked anxiously.

"No," he said. He linked his fingers behind my neck. "Rhonnie . . . honey, all I want is for you to be happy. That's all I want."

His heart was bared to me in his face. My throat swelled up. Then Sophie tried to open the door. My father opened it for her. She gave us both an admonishing look.

"The madam says I must tell you the coffee will be cold."

"Is she cross?" asked my father. "Tell her we're coming."

"I'm cross," Sophie informed him, stumping towards the outside door. "I'm supposed to finish at two o'clock. I can't wash the cups now. The cups must wait like the children of Israel. I'm too late already."

"Right, off you go, then," my father said mildly. "Have a nice time in church. Don't forget to pray for me."

Her head reappeared round the doorjamb. "Always, master. Always I must pray for you. Always I must pray for all the family in this house," she said in a resigned tone. And she scurried across the yard to her room.

"Poor Sophie. Hell, it's a tough life, hey, Rhonnie?"

He tucked my arm through his, and we walked into the passage. I drew up, suddenly, in mid stride.

"Dad, I love you," I told him.

He unhooked his arm and faced me. Straightening his shoulders, he took a deep breath and let it out again. It was quite shadowy where we were standing, so I couldn't be sure, but his eyes seemed to have a wet shine to them.

"Thank you," he said in a hoarse whisper. Then he walked on quickly, leaving me behind.

Helen and Victor were sitting on the sun-loungers in a shaded corner of the patio, reading the *Sunday Express*. My father poured himself a cup of coffee, sank into a chair, and concealed himself behind the *Sunday Times*. My mother was a little way down the garden, inspecting a bed of newly planted seedlings.

I had a moment of panic until I saw Dave. He was lying stretched out on the edge of the swimming pool. I went up to him quietly. He appeared to be fast asleep, so I backed off and sat down to watch him. I was feeling rather choked up, and glad not to have to talk.

But he wasn't asleep. After a minute, I discovered that he was peeping at me from under his elbow.

"Hi," I said.

"Fancy a smoke? They're in my top pocket. Light one for me, will you? My hand's wet."

"Lazy sod. I thought you were asleep," I accused him.

He smiled up at me indolently as I stuck the lit cigarette

between his lips. "I've been waiting for you to come and provide a pillow for my head."

"Men! You expect to be waited on hand and foot."

"No, just my head. That'll do for now."

I nudged him in the side with my sandal before I obligingly settled myself down in the right position. He moved his head onto my lap. Letting out a smoky sigh of satisfaction, he closed his eyes. I glanced towards the patio. Nobody was observing us. Hesitantly, I touched his forehead and began to stroke my fingers over the top of his skull. It was a weird sensation; I didn't like it; I wanted to be caressing hair, not skin.

"Mmm . . ." he murmured.

"Dave? Can I ask you something?"

"What?"

"Will you tell me why you shave your head?"

One eye opened a crack. "Is that a complaint?"

"No—not really. Well . . ." My father was right, I thought: If you loved someone, you had to be able to be honest with them. "Maybe it is a complaint," I confessed apprehensively. "I'd like to see you with hair."

"You wouldn't," he said, and shut his eye.

"I wouldn't? Why, what's wrong with your hair?"

No answer came. There was a flicker of movement under his lids, and a muscle in his jaw clenched. Prodding him, I repeated my question.

He said, "I don't know how to explain this—my great-grandfather . . . he had—he had a thing about porcupines. I mean . . . actually, I guess you'd call him a sexual masochist. He used to take them to bed with him." The

94

creases on either side of his mouth twitched in a fleeting hint of amusement.

"This is all very interesting, Dave, but what's it got to do—"

"I'm trying to explain! You see, I have porcupine genes in my ancestry. That's what's wrong with my hair. It grows in quills, and it doesn't grow out—it shoots out. I quilled the first girl I made love to."

"Very funny!" I said.

I leaned back on my hands, beyond his range of vision. He carried on smoking, lying otherwise dead still and quiet. After an eternity of silence, he spoke my name softly, tentatively.

"Ya?" I said sulkily.

"Rhonda . . . ?" His hand came up, felt over my knee, along the outside of my thigh. "Rhonda? I love you, Rhonda."

I was won over, but not prepared to let him know it, yet. I stayed mute. Suddenly he sat up. Pivoting round on his bottom, he flicked the stub of his cigarette away, grinned, and pounced, tickling me all over.

"Hey, do *you* love *me*?" he demanded.

"D-o-on't!" I screeched. "Plee-ee . . . I'm terribly tick—"

"Do you?"

"Yes—ye-es . . . anything—plee—"

"Say it."

"I lo-huv . . . you, Da-a-ve."

His fingers stilled. We sat, entangled, breathing heavily, gazing into each other's eyes. His mouth inched closer.

Nervously, my glance went towards the patio; I caught the movement of four faces being turned away quickly.

"Oh dear," I whispered, "we're being watched."

"Oh hell. I wanted to kiss you."

"It's all right. They're not looking now."

But he didn't kiss me. We had both become shy and embarrassed. He disentangled himself from me, straightened his clothes, and stretched out on his side. I fiddled with the clasp on the silver Victorian locket that my grandmother had given me, and which was one of my most cherished possessions.

"What's that?" he asked.

"Your shell." I got it out of the locket and handed it to him. "I want you to explain its significance. You promised you would, remember?"

"There's nothing to explain. . . . All right, I'll show you."

His hand and my shell disappeared briefly into his pocket. Then he held out his fist and opened it. On the palm were two cowries, identical in shape, and color, and size. I couldn't tell them apart.

"Which is mine?" I asked.

"It doesn't matter." He picked one up and gave it to me, and shoved the other back in his pocket. "Satisfied?"

"No," I said. "I still don't understand."

"Don't try. You'll understand one day."

Half joking, I asked, "Dave, is this some kind of witchcraft? You haven't cast a spell on me, have you?"

"If I had, we wouldn't be sitting here now."

"Where would we be?"

"On my Honda, heading into the sunset."

"Heading for where, exactly?"

"The trouble with you," he said, "is that you have no imagination. I'm going to sleep. I'm clapped out; I only got to bed at two." He lay down on his back, positioning himself so that his head rested on my thigh. "Comfy?" he asked.

"Why did you get to bed so late?" I said suspiciously.

He had shut his eyes. He was smiling, as if he knew he had aroused my jealousy and was enjoying keeping me in suspense.

"Dave! You told me you would be helping your father deliver a few pieces of furniture yesterday evening."

"Ya, I did. That's what *I* did last night. What did *you* do? Did you see . . . what's-his-name? . . . Brian?"

"Brian? Who mentioned—" I began to laugh. "Oh, you needn't worry about Brian."

His smile spread briefly into a smug grin. Within a few seconds he had dozed off.

I was happy, sitting there in the sun beside the swimming pool, studying Dave's face lovingly while he slept. I knew, without knowing how I knew, that this time—for the first time in my life—what I was feeling was real.

nine

September. Springtime in Johannesburg. Blossom time. And I was in love, and the sun seemed to shine every day especially for us. Dave and me. *Us.* Finally, I was able to understand the significance of the shells, after I asked Dave where he had got them.

It was an afternoon during the week. We were relaxing in our bathing suits, dabbling our toes in the swimming pool while we digested the sandwiches and iced pineapple juice Sophie had brought out to us on a tray.

"I found them on a beach," he said.

"A beach where?"

"In the Cape. There were millions of them."

"Beaches?" I was in a silly, giggly mood.

"Don't be so dense." He splashed some water at me.

"Millions of shells, cowries. Quite a few rare ones too."

"Is the one you gave me rare?"

"Hardly. Don't you know anything about cowries?"

"No. Is it a very common sort?"

"Very, so I wouldn't make a fuss over it."

A large dragonfly appeared out of the blue and hovered momentarily in the air in front of me. I squinted at it, thinking. As it banked steeply and skimmed away into the glare, the sun struck a rainbow dazzle of light off its wings.

"Dave, the shells—they're us, aren't they?"

"Us?" he said, visibly embarrassed; and he launched himself into the water, drenching me in a cold shower of spray.

I smiled to myself. My Dave. My funny Dave was an old-fashioned romantic at heart. The discovery delighted me.

A little later, the same day, I discovered something else about Dave, something about his past that enabled me to understand him much better.

Mark was being a nuisance. He had come along and caught us kissing in the pool. After putting on his performance of retching and choking with disgust, he took a running jump into the water, landing nearly on top of us. I left Dave to deal with him, and climbed out. When the pair of them eventually emerged, shivering and grinning, my inconsiderate small beast of a brother plonked himself down on his towel between Dave and me.

"Do you mind?" I said, glowering at him. "We don't want you here, Mark."

"Too bad!" He folded his arms over his skinny chest. "I bet—hey, Dave—I bet you didn't know you can die from kissing. True's bob. You swallow a lot of germs. I know a chap who's in the army and he told me about this infantryman who died after he'd kissed—"

"Shut up, Mark. And beat it! Now! . . . I'm warning you," I said.

"You can't make me. You don't own this pool. I can sit here if I want to."

"I wouldn't if I were you," Dave told him. "Not if you value your life."

"Why? You going to throw me in?" Mark asked hopefully. "You can't throw me in, Dave. You're too puny, man."

"It's your funeral," said Dave. "If you want to die from our germs, fair enough." Pursing his lips, he leaned across Mark and pretended to kiss me.

With alacrity, squealing, Mark removed himself and his towel. But he settled down again less than a yard away.

As a last resort, I tried pleading with him. "Please, Markie. Be decent, huh? Give us a break. Go and lie on the other side of the pool."

"No. It's not so hot there. It's farther away from the sun."

"I'm sorry. We'll just have to ignore him," I told Dave in an exasperated tone.

Immediately, Mark said, "Okay, if you want me to vamoose, I will. But it'll cost you."

"How much?" Dave asked.

"Don't," I said. "Ignore him, Dave. Don't encourage him."

"Fifty cents," said Mark.

"Ten cents," said Dave. "I'll pay you later. Deal?"

"Deal," said Mark. He whipped up his towel, whistled for J.R., who was lolling in the shade, and went haring off down the garden.

"You shouldn't have done that," I grumbled. "It'll only make him worse."

Receiving no answer, I turned. Dave was sitting in a huddled position, knees drawn up under his chin, forearms hugging his ankles. With an intent gaze, he was watching Mark and J.R. having a tug-of-war over Mark's towel on the lawn.

"He's so damn like my brother!" Flopping back, he rolled onto his stomach and covered his face with his arms.

"Your brother?" I stared, mouth agape, at the sunburned shine on his head. Dimly, somewhere in my shocked mind, I registered the thought that he ought to be wearing a hat. "Did you say your brother? But you don't have a brother. . . . Dave!" I grasped his shoulder and shook it. "You told me you were an only child."

Raising himself onto his knees, he stood up and went to fetch his cigarettes and matches from where he had left them at the end of the pool. Lighting a cigarette, he offered it to me. As I pushed his hand away, I detected that same unaccountable expression of torment in his eyes I had caught glimpses of before. Then his face closed up.

"I am an only child," he told me in a leaden voice.

"So why did you say that Mark—"

"I *had* a brother—when I was much younger . . . and two sisters." He grimaced, sucking in smoke. "Not anymore. They're dead." And he stepped over my ankles and sat down with his back to me.

"God, I didn't know," I stammered, full of remorse. "I'm so sorry, Dave."

His shoulders moved up and down in a shrug. I stretched out and touched him.

"How did they—do you want to talk about it? Will it help to tell me?"

"No, it won't help. Look, just forget it," he said. "It doesn't matter. It's all over and done with. It's in the past."

I slid closer to him and laid my cheek against his shoulder. It wasn't all over and done with, or he would have been able to talk about it. I understood, now, his reticence on the subject of his family and his upbringing; those haunted looks of his; the sudden withdrawals into himself. Hugging him, I felt his pain.

"I love you, Dave," I said fiercely, and kissed him.

And with a wonderful sense of timing, my mother chose that particular moment to come out and call us to tea.

ten

Mark turned nine in the third week of September. A few days before his birthday, J.R. was run over by a car and killed right outside our front gate. The driver of the car didn't even bother to stop.

Dave and I arrived home from college only seconds after the accident happened. J.R. was lying in the middle of the road. Mark was crouched over him. A large silver Mercedes was cruising away from the scene. It accelerated and quickly disappeared; at the same time, Mark straightened up, saw us, and started screaming.

Dave pulled me off the bike, let it fall sideways on the grassy curb, and raced into the road. Quaking with dread, I followed. I knew J.R. was dead. I could see, without allowing myself to look at him directly, that he had a large deep gash across the top of his head and that he wasn't breathing. While Dave was examining him, I tried to comfort Mark. But he fought me off with his fists. He was hysterical.

"I'll kill him! I'll kill him! The bloody murderer! He didn't stop. I'll kill him!"

His yelling brought my mother and Sophie flying down the drive. I've never seen either one of them run so fast.

"Ah no," my mother gasped. "Ah no, is it J.R.? Is he . . . ?"

Dave stood up. There was blood on his hands. He muttered, "It's no use. His skull's . . . At least he didn't suffer. He must have died inst—"

"NO-OO!" Mark's scream cut him off. "He's NOT dead. He's NOT! We've got to take him to the vet. The vet'll do something. We've got to take him. *Please! Please!* We've got to!" He dropped down on his knees in the road.

"We will," Dave said at once. "Come on, we'll take him on the bike. It'll be quickest." And while the rest of us stood frozen in a state of shock, he gently scooped up J.R.'s broken body and ran, with Mark at his side, to the Honda.

In a matter of seconds they were gone. They were already out of sight when my mother recovered her voice.

"Tell them to come back. They must come back. Mark's not wearing a crash helmet. He might fall off."

Sophie, hands up to her face, was staring at the sticky red stain on the road. "Au, au, au, Miss Rhonda. Dead. Au shame. Au shame, madam. Shame for everybody." And she burst into tears.

I dodged past her, darted through the gate, up the drive, and into the house. I thought I was going to be sick, but the feeling of nausea subsided when I reached the bathroom. I sat on the edge of the tub for a while. Then I heard my mother and Sophie in the kitchen. I didn't want to be with them, so I slunk into my bedroom, closed the door, and listened at the window for the sound of Dave and Mark's return.

They brought J.R.'s body back with them. Mark was determined that J.R. should have a decent burial, with a proper ceremony, which he asked Dave to conduct. Dave dug the grave at the bottom of the garden under the mulberry tree, conducted the ceremony, filled in the grave, and spent a further hour fashioning a cross out of the legs of an old wooden stool Mark found in the garden shed. Mark raided my mother's flower beds for a wreath to lay on the grave. My mother watched him doing it, without saying a word. She called me into the kitchen to collect the tea she had prepared for us.

"Where's Sophie?" I asked her.

"She's in her room. I told her I'd take over here. I can't have her breaking into tears in front of Mark. How is he?"

"He's all right. Dave's looking after him. They're carving an inscription on the cross."

"Poor little J.R.," my mother said.

The numbness inside me flared up into a smarting pressure at the back of my throat; I bit hard on my teeth. My mother shooed a fly off the sugar bowl.

"How on earth did it happen? I've warned Mark so

many times never to let J.R. out in the street, except on a lead. Were you there? Did you actually see it happen, Rhonda?"

"No," I rasped. "Is the tray ready now? Can I take—"

"What I fail to understand is why the driver didn't stop, even if it wasn't his fault. I suppose it was an African. It must have been. I'm sure a White person would—"

"It was a White person." I snatched up the tray. "Mark said he was middle-aged, with gray hair, and smartly dressed. And he was driving a ruddy great Mercedes. We saw the car. It took off like the clappers as soon as we appeared. No doubt the swine thought we were going to pursue him. I wish to God we had."

"Mind! Watch the tray. You're spilling the milk."

"I wish we had gone after him. I'd like to wring his neck."

"It's terrible. Poor little J.R."

My eyes shied away from hers; my vision was beginning to blur. I stumbled past her to the door.

"Rhonda . . ."

"What?" I said gruffly. It was hopeless; we couldn't comfort each other.

"I need to lie down for a bit. Will you keep an eye on Mark? . . . And Rhonda? . . . Rhonda, will you please tell Dave I'm grateful to him. He has been very helpful. He's a nice lad."

I felt that to be the understatement of the year. But then, coming from my mother, it meant quite a lot. She hadn't really been able to bring herself to approve of Dave up until now.

My "nice lad" was sprawled, relaxing, in the middle of the lawn. He was alone; Mark wasn't anywhere to be seen. I composed myself on the patio before I went to join him. He looked utterly worn out; his face had a waxy pallor, streaked by lines of dried sweat and dirt.

"I've brought you some tea. Also a cold beer, in case you want one. Where's Mark got to?"

Dave opened the can of lager and gulped from it thirstily. "He's cycling around the neighborhood, searching for the Mercedes. He thinks the guy must live locally."

"I hope we find him."

"Why? What'll you do then?"

"Do?"

"To the guy? What can you do?"

"I'll kill him," I said with incensed passion.

Dave shrugged wearily. "He isn't that unusual, you know. Lots of people don't stop when they run over animals in the road."

"Not *White* people!" I erupted in a blind fury of emotion. "Not when they run over somebody's pet dog."

My outburst had a peculiar effect on him; he froze, and a tide of blood colored his cheeks. "Is that what you think?" Lighting a cigarette, he held the burning match between finger and thumb, watching the stick blacken and bend as the flame advanced. "You reckon White people are more moral than anyone else? You reckon Apartheid is moral, then, do you?"

"Apartheid? What's that got to—hey! Watch it, you'll burn your fingers."

I blew out the match. He immediately struck another.

107

Shielding it with his hand, he gazed at me tensely. Then he shook his head and smiled. His smile wasn't genuine, though—it chilled me.

"Black and White don't mix, do they? Look, see what happens to this matchstick." He held it up between us; the flame flickered and died. "Blast!" he muttered.

"What are you trying to show me?" I asked him.

"Forget it." He got up stiffly. "Say good-bye to Mark for me."

"You're not going?"

"I've got two essays to write."

Something was wrong, I knew. He wouldn't even look at me as he brushed the grass off his trousers and buttoned up his shirt. I fought desperately against a consuming feeling of wretchedness. Dave was rubbing at a dark mark on the cuff of his sleeve. I stared at it. It was a bloodstain. J.R.'s blood. A vision of J.R.'s body lying in the road swam before my eyes. Then I saw him racing down the drive to meet me, with his ridiculous floppy ears streamlined and his little legs working at full speed. The reality sank in: J.R. was dead. *Dead.* Without any warning, the dam inside me burst.

I felt Dave's arms close round my shoulders. I hung on to him while I cried myself out. When I was able to speak, I gulped, "I'm sorry . . . it's . . ."

"J.R. I understand," he mumbled. "It's a terrible shock."

"He wasn't even two years old. It seems so unfair. He wasn't even grown up. He had such a short life."

"Short, but happy. He was lucky, really."

108

"You think so?"

"He wasn't kicked. He never went hungry. He didn't ever suffer. And he isn't suffering now. You're the one who's suffering."

He had made me smile guiltily. I snuggled my cheek against his chest. "You're lovely." I sighed. "I don't know what I'd do without you."

His hold on me slackened abruptly.

Anxiously, I asked, "Are you still upset with me?"

"Upset?"

"I felt you were cross with me earlier for what I said about White drivers. But, you know, I didn't mean to sound—I haven't got anything against Blacks. I'm not really prejudiced. And in case it bothers you, to answer your question: I wouldn't try to claim Apartheid is moral, only . . ." I listened to his heartbeat for several seconds. "Well, I guess I have to admit that I'm just not all that interested in politics. Are you?"

"No," he said gruffly, after a short silence. He let out a shuddery laugh. "Live for the moment, that's the answer."

I craned my neck to look at him. "To what, Dave?"

"Today. J.R. It makes you think. You never know when your number is going to come up, so it's probably stupid to worry about the future. I mean, we could both be dead tomorrow. I could be flattened by a bus on my way home from—"

"Don't!"

I clutched him to me. He hugged me very tightly. Then he kissed the top of my head, and broke free.

"I *must* go. As well as these two essays, I've also got a lot of other stuff to prepare for next week."

"Next week?" I did my best to smile. "That's worrying about the future."

He gave me a strange, sad look. "God, I wish—I only wish I didn't have to," he said.

eleven

Mark's birthday fell on a Saturday. My mother had told him he could have a *smallish* party in the afternoon. He interpreted that very liberally and invited his whole class from school. He also invited Dave. Unfortunately—or perhaps fortunately for Dave, he couldn't accept because he worked all day on Saturdays. But he told Mark he would see him after the party. Mark promised to save him a piece of birthday cake.

At midday I was in the kitchen, helping prepare the sickly feast that was going to be laid out later on a trestle table in the garden. I heard a motorbike pull up outside, and from the sound of the engine, I knew it was Dave, even though I wasn't expecting him. I ran to greet him.

"What are you doing here?" I asked gleefully. "Aren't

you supposed to be working?" I was so thrilled to see him that it didn't even strike me as odd that he was wearing a bulky anorak, zipped up to the neck, on a day when I was feeling hot and sweaty in my bikini top and shorts.

He grinned at me, holding his arms crossed in front of him. "Where's Mark?"

"In his bedroom, I think. He was there a little while ago. He's somewhere around. Why?"

"I've brought him a birthday present."

"You have?"

He unzipped the anorak a few inches. Something bulged under the padded nylon, and a small black, shiny nose appeared. Two frightened dark eyes, the size of shirt buttons, peeped out at me.

"Oh Dave, is it a puppy?"

He reached his hand inside the opening and brought out a quivering ball of fur. Four woolly paws and a spiky tail dangled down between his fingers. A white ruff surrounded the wet licorice nose. The puppy's head was velvety black, the rest of its body fluffy white.

"Can I hold it?" I pleaded.

He transferred the puppy into my arms and, with a self-satisfied smirk, watched me gushing over it.

"Do you think Mark will like it?" he asked.

"How could he possibly not?" I gazed up at him, overcome. "You are . . . I'm stuck for words. . . . You're just too much, you know that?"

"Who are you talking to? The puppy?"

As I was about to answer, Mark shot into sight round the side of the house.

112

"Hey! Dave!" he yelled, waving his pellet gun up in the air. "Hey, look what I've got."

Dave snatched the puppy from me. He turned only when Mark was almost upon him. "Hi, Mark," he said casually.

Mark's eyes bulged. His mouth dropped open. He goggled at the puppy as if he couldn't believe his senses.

"That's a nice rifle," Dave said.

Carelessly, Mark dropped the gun on the ground and stretched up to stroke the furry little face that was peeking out nervously from the crook of Dave's elbow.

"Wh-whose puppy is it? Is it . . . yours?"

"No, it belongs to a friend of mine," said Dave. "I'm only looking after it. Would you like to hold it?" Before he finished his question, Mark had already taken the puppy from him.

"He's so soft," Mark spluttered. His face was pink with emotion.

"You like him?" Dave asked superfluously.

With his head bent, Mark nodded. "What does your friend call him?"

"That's for you to decide," Dave said. "It's your dog. Happy Birthday."

Mark looked up. "You're giving him to me?"

"Yup. Unless you don't want him because he's not a he, he's a she. Do you mind?"

"A she? You sure?" Mark looked for himself. "Oh." He was clearly disappointed. "Never mind," he said. "She can't help being a girl."

He lifted the puppy up to his face and touched noses

113

with it. A tiny pink tongue came out and licked him experimentally. Then the spiky tail started to wag.

Mark's eyes filled. "See . . ." He emitted a choking sound. "See . . . she loves me already." Clutching the squirming puppy to his chest, he broke into a run.

"Mark—hey, where are you going?" I shouted.

"To show Mom. Come on."

By then he was out of earshot. I turned to Dave, shaking my head apologetically. "He didn't even thank you."

"He did," said Dave, beaming. "But I'm not sure your mother will."

"Oh, she won't mind. And if she does—too bad! It's a fait accompli. There's nothing she can do about it, except maybe grumble a bit."

"Thanks. That's very reassuring! I think I'll just vamoose now before—"

"No, you don't, you coward. Come along." I got a firm hold on his arm and tugged him after me into the house.

An encouraging sight met our eyes in the kitchen. My mother and Sophie were exclaiming over the new addition to our family with maternal clucks and melting expressions. Sophie was smiling wide enough to reveal the missing molars at the back of her mouth.

"My baby, my baby . . . au, Master Mark, he's too little, isn't it?"

"He's quite adorable," my mother said. "Where does he come from, Mark?"

"From Dave," said Mark, and then my mother looked round and saw us standing in the doorway. "But he's not a boy, Mom, he's a girl."

"She's very sweet," my mother said to Dave. "What breed is she?"

"She's . . . uh . . ." Dave glanced at me. "She's a . . . spaniel?" he suggested hopefully.

My mother's eyebrows lifted. "Surely not. She can't be. She's too fluffy."

"Poodle, then?" Dave said.

"I don't believe you." My mother laughed.

"No, well, actually, her father's a poodle, and her mother's a spaniel, and she—she's a mistake, really."

"She isn't!" Mark said stoutly. "She's not a mistake. She's a spoodle."

"That's right," said Dave. "That's what she is."

"I must say she doesn't *look* like a mongrel," my mother said. "She's such a pretty little puppy. Put her down, Mark, so we can see her properly. What do you call her, Dave?"

Dave looked at me. I looked at my mother. Mark straightened up from crouching on the floor.

"I think I'll call her Spoodie," he announced, unaware of the sudden tension in the room.

My mother's smile had shrunk. I decided I had better say something.

"Didn't Mark tell you, Mom, the puppy is a birthday present from Dave?"

"My gun! I forgot my gun!" Mark screeched. "Watch Spoodie for me, Sophie."

His dash from the kitchen frightened the puppy. She tried to hide between my mother's feet. My mother bent down to comfort her. I made a thumbs-up victory sign to

115

Dave; then I saw that Sophie was scowling and shaking her head.

"What's the matter?" I asked her.

"That one isn't coming to live here, Miss Rhonda."

"The puppy? Why not, Sophie? I thought you liked it."

"Not in this house. Not to live here. You tell me, Miss Rhonda, who must look after it? Who must clean up all the mess? If you think the Lord—"

"Never mind all that now, Sophie," my mother said smartly, brushing down her skirt. "It's Mark's dog. He must look after it. Obviously this isn't the most convenient time, but we'll manage somehow. So long as it's—I presume it *is* house-trained, Dave?"

Dave started to answer; a loud squawk from Sophie cut him off. My mother stepped back swiftly. The puppy was squatting, and a pool of water was spreading out from under the feathery quill of a tail.

"Yes . . . well . . ." Dave said. He gave my mother a sheepish grin. "Uh . . . if you'll excuse me, I've got to get back to work." And he fled.

twelve

That evening Dave took me to a party. All I knew in advance was that it was being given by somebody called Gavin, who lived only a few blocks away from Dave in Turffontein.

We set off from my house in a celebratory mood. When we got to Hillbrow, Dave suggested we should stop and have a drink. He had a beer and I had a glass of white wine. As we sat in the hotel lounge, holding hands and cracking silly jokes and laughing at nothing, other people in the room kept looking round at us. Dave's shaved head always attracted some attention in public, but on this occasion I felt people were drawn to us because we were so obviously happy together. I grinned at them charitably, and they grinned back. After this had happened three or four times, Dave asked me whom I was smiling at. The wine had gone to my head; I felt bubbly and frivolous.

Teasingly, I said, "Never you mind."

"I want to know."

"Why?" I said, laughing.

"Were you smiling at *him*?"

"Him? Who are you talking about?"

"Over there." He jerked his thumb. "The preening peacock who can't keep his eyes off you."

I glanced across at the specimen in question. I had noticed him before—he was handsome in a flashy, overdressed manner. Intercepting my glance, he raised his glass to me, and I smiled back without thinking.

Dave's reaction was as surprising as it was sudden. He snatched his hand from mine and sprang to his feet.

"Well, if you fancy him, don't let me stop you from joining him. I'm going to the gents'," he said, and walked out.

He had finished his beer. My own glass was empty and I was aware of curious eyes trained on me. Grabbing up my coat, I went to wait for him in the lobby.

"What's got into you?" I demanded as soon as he came through the swing door. "Why did you react like that just now?"

"I don't like flirts," he said.

There were people all around us. I tried to lower my voice. "I am *not* a flirt."

We glowered at each other. A passing couple twisted their necks, staring curiously.

"Come on," Dave said finally, "we'd better clear out of here."

118

We didn't speak until we reached the bike. Then he asked me if I still wanted to go to the party.

Resentfully, I muttered, "Do *you*?"

He shrugged and mounted the bike, leaving me to clamber up on my own.

And that was only the prelude to what turned out to be a disastrous evening.

The party was awful! I had hoped to meet some of Dave's friends, but he didn't introduce me to anyone except Gavin, who opened the door to us. Gavin was tall and lanky, with gray eyes and longish, straggly red hair. I liked him. He amused me with small talk in the hallway while Dave disappeared into the kitchen to fetch drinks for us. We had to stand in the hallway because there was nowhere else to stand. The small house was jam-packed with people. The noise was tremendous; Gavin and I had to shout into each other's ears to be heard. In the room adjoining the hall, rock music was being played at full blast. I could feel the floorboards under my feet reverberating; the wall behind me seemed to be vibrating as well.

Dave returned with a glass of wine. He thrust it at me, said something about needing to talk to someone, and promptly disappeared again. Then Gavin's girlfriend popped up out of the crush. She gave me a spiteful look—as if she suspected me of trying to take him from her—and carted him off to dance. I was alone. But not for long.

A seedy character attempted to pick me up. He was drunk and obnoxious, and I couldn't get rid of him. I couldn't escape from him, either, because he had me pinned

119

against the wall between his arms. I was praying for Dave to come and rescue me. He appeared for a moment, saw what was happening—and vanished. I presumed he thought that I was enjoying myself, that I was flirting! I felt furious with him then. And I was thankful when a beefy rugby player type squeezed forward and asked me if I was having trouble. At a nod from me, he sent the drunk packing and introduced himself.

Ian, his name was. He tested sports equipment for a living. Sports, I gathered, were his whole life. He quickly muscled through the crowd to refill my glass, then proceeded to tell me all about himself. I only heard half of what he said, but it didn't seem to matter. He evidently enjoyed the sound of his own voice. Out of gratitude, I agreed to go and dance with him. There was more space to move around in now, as the supply of alcohol had run out and people were starting to leave.

After one dance, Ian changed the record and turned the volume down. Somebody else switched off the lights in the room. I told myself that it was all over between Dave and me and I didn't care.

I snuggled in close against Ian. He had arms like a gorilla; I felt as if I were being smothered, but I smiled up at him. He maneuvered me into a corner and kissed me. The earth moved—unpleasantly. I had had too much to drink. I turned my head for some air, and saw Dave. He was standing at the door, facing my way. Although the room was in darkness, I knew I was visible to him. And I knew he must have seen the kiss. But he wasn't angry. Against the blaze of light in the hallway behind him, his face was a bloodless, sickly color. He looked hurt, deeply hurt, and utterly wretched.

Ian was trying to kiss me again. I struggled with him. When I glanced back at the doorway, it was empty.

"Come outside," Ian urged.

"Let me go," I hissed at him.

"No, give me another kiss first."

I freed myself by digging my elbows into his stomach. Dave wasn't in the hallway. I ran into the kitchen. The back door was open. I found him sitting on the step outside.

"Oh . . . hi," I said.

He peered past me into the kitchen. "You alone?"

"Yes . . . Da—"

"I'm thinking of pushing off now." He got to his feet. "Did you want a lift?"

"Please. If you don't mind?"

"No, I don't mind."

We were being so horribly formal and polite to each other. He fetched my coat. Gavin had taken his girlfriend home, so Dave left him a note on the kitchen table, and we slipped out the back way.

"There's a path round the side of the house. But watch your step," he warned. "It's hellish dark."

A moment later he tripped over the dustbin and went sprawling. I dashed to his aid and fell over his feet, and landed on top of him. When we realized we weren't hurt, we starting laughing.

"Damn dustbin." He gave it a kick as he helped me up. "It must be drunk."

121

"You are," I said.

"No, I'm not. I can't see a blessed thing, though. Can you?"

"Not a thing," I lied.

It wasn't that dark. I could discern his profile, and the white of his eye. He was looking at me without turning his head. I felt his hesitation, and made myself shiver.

"It's quite spooky, isn't it, Dave?"

His hand immediately groped for mine. I slid my fingers into his and squeezed. He squeezed back.

"Hold on to me," he said. "I'll go first. If a spook grabs me, you run like hell."

"Don't," I said. He laughed, and I felt a lot happier suddenly.

He released my hand only when we were safely out in the street. "I wouldn't mind a cup of coffee," he said then. "How about you?"

"Could we have one at your house? You live near here . . . not so?"

"Ya, I do." He fiddled with the mirror on the bike's handlebar.

"I've never been to your house," I said. "It would be nice to see where you live."

"Sure, I'll show you. I'll give you the grand tour of Turffontein if you like. I'll show you the racecourse and—"

"Just your house, please. Save the grand tour for when it's daylight."

"I'll *show* you my house, but I'm sorry, I can't invite you in for coffee at this hour. My parents go to bed early. We'd wake them up."

122

"Would we disturb them, even if we were very quiet?"

"Their bedroom is right next to the kitchen."

"Okay. Too bad. Forget the coffee," I said crustily. I was unreasonably hurt. "Just take me home."

He parked the Honda at the front gate as usual and walked me up the drive. I dug my key out of my purse and unlocked the front door.

"Thank you for the lift," I muttered.

He cleared his throat. I waited. The house was silent. The only sound was a faint intermittent chirping from a tired cricket, hidden somewhere in the inky blackness of the garden.

Curtly I said, "Well, good night."

" 'Night."

I pushed the door open.

"Rh . . . wait!"

He caught my arm and pulled me back. The hall light left me temporarily blind. A warm object bumped my nose, then his mouth pressed against mine. I resisted.

"Rhonda . . . ?"

He clasped me more gently, and I started to relax. I put my arms round him. I wanted him to hold me, to hug me. Hugs are healing; and they can be a way of saying you're sorry when the actual words stick in your throat.

It was all I wanted from him that evening—a hug. He kissed me. Then his hand slid round under my arm and grasped my breast.

"No!" I gasped, and shoved him.

I had used more force than I had intended; he was sent reeling back before he righted himself. His face contorted in anger.

"Don't tell me that isn't what *you* wanted!"

"*I* wanted? How dare you . . . !" I had to restrain myself from hitting him. First the drunk, then Ian, now . . . Dave! Dave as well! And I had thought he was different! "You . . . ! You beast!" I spat at him. "I never want to see you again." I dived inside, locked the door, slammed the bolts home, switched off the light, and fled down the dark passage to my bedroom.

I lay on my bed, fully clothed. I lay there a long time. When my fury left me, the hard, painful lump in my chest prevented me from falling asleep. At some point I got up, put on my pajamas, and washed my face in the bathroom. I made a bit of noise, hoping my father would wake up. I needed to talk to him. But he continued snoring; I could hear him through the bathroom wall.

Mark's bedroom door was closed. I opened it quietly and went in. The floor was covered with newspaper. I picked my way round the messes and puddles. The glow from the night-light next to the bed showed me that there were two heads on the pillow. One of them was small and furry and producing little snuffly sounds in its sleep. Mark's face was turned towards the puppy—their noses were virtually touching—and his arm was clutching the puppy's body under the blanket.

As I stood and gazed down at them, the lump in my chest moved up and blocked my throat. A jumble of feelings came to the surface. I hadn't known I possessed a maternal streak until now; but this feeling, even distinct as it was, couldn't be separated from the other feelings, all of which centered on Dave.

Oh hell, I am *in love with him,* I thought miserably, and the tears started. I wept silently, so as not to disturb Mark and his live teddy bear. I wished I could climb into bed with them, but then I would have had to explain my presence in the morning.

Back in my own bed, I hugged my pillow. It was a poor substitute for a warm puppy. Had I been given a choice, however, it wasn't the puppy that I would have chosen to share my bed. I could still feel Dave's hand on my breast, and that was part of the reason I didn't fall asleep for another hour.

thirteen

Mark woke me shortly after eight. I prized my eyes open a crack. They felt swollen and sore.

"Go away," I mumbled, and rolled onto my other side.

"No. Wake up!"

He pinched me. I swore at him, and pulled the sheet over my head. He ripped it back.

"Please. Come on. Wake up. You must. Please!"

The appeal got through to me. I lifted my head and peered at him muzzily.

"Why must I—what is it, Mark? What's the matter?"

"Spoodie," he said. "I think she's hurt."

"Oh God, no." I shot out of bed. "Where is she? In your room?"

"She's outside. You'd better put your gown on." He fetched it for me from the back of the door. "It's okay, you needn't hurry too much. She's not badly hurt. She's not dying or anything, I mean."

"Well, what's wrong with her? Where are Mom and Dad? Have you told them?"

"Sshh!" he warned as I followed him into the passage. "Their door's shut. They're sleeping, and I didn't want to worry them. I thought it best if you have a look at her first. She's just down near the gate."

"The gate?" I walked faster. "What the hell's she doing down there? You shouldn't have left—"

"I had to. She can't move," he said.

"Can't *move*?" I dashed ahead of him to the top of the driveway. The front gate was wide open. "Mark!" I cried in panic. "Where is she?"

He squealed. "She's gone. She must be in the road. Quick! Run!"

I was already sprinting. Hitching up my gown above my knees, I pelted down the drive and out the gate. On the sidewalk stood a motorbike. Behind it, a figure sat slumped in the shade under the front hedge. I gasped.

"You . . . ?"

"I'm afraid so." He tottered to his feet. "I'm sorry, but I had to talk to you."

"What's going—" I spun round. "Mark . . . !" I shouted, and glimpsed a flash of movement as he vanished back into the house. As understanding slowly dawned on me, my mouth dropped open. I gawked at Dave. "And Spoodie?" I said.

127

He grimaced. "Ya, I know. It was a mean trick. But it was the only way Mark could think of getting you out here. I didn't want him to tell you it was me."

"Why not?" My brain wasn't functioning too well; half of it was still asleep, the other half recovering from shock.

"I was scared you wouldn't come if you knew."

"Oh," I said. Then I took in what he was wearing. "Dave—have you been sitting here all night?"

"Yup." He grinned shamefacedly.

"The *whole* night?"

"Yup."

"Why? I mean, didn't you . . . ?" I was flabbergasted. "Why, Dave?"

He just looked at me, his eyes bloodshot and underlined with black smudges of fatigue. His expression conveyed more to me than anything he could have said. I went to him. He rested his hands on my shoulders, leaning against me. Our foreheads touched. My hair screened us from the outside world.

"It hurts," he admitted.

"I *know*." His pain was a part of mine.

"I'm sorry about last night. I'm truly sorry."

"So am I. It wasn't only your fault. We got our wires crossed."

He laughed; in his exhaustion, it was an effort. "You know what the trouble is with me? I'm so darn jealous."

"I'm glad. I am too. I can't stand the thought of you being with anybody else." I hugged him; his body felt thinner than usual, bonier, more fragile.

"Ruddy sex," he said. "It always complicates things. I've been thinking—a lot, all night."

"Thinking about what, Dave?"

"Us, I guess—mainly. I reckon it's probably wisest to go on as we are."

"As we are? I'm not sure I understand—"

"No. I'm not sure I do, either. I'm too tired now. I can't think clearly anymore. All I know is . . . I just couldn't bear to lose you, that's all."

"You can't!" I assured him. "You can't lose me. You're stuck with me, Dave. I love you."

He stood back and gazed at me wearily through half-closed, puffy lids. A slow grin eased the suffering from his face. "I like what you're wearing," he said.

I had clean forgotten that I wasn't decently dressed. My pajamas were thin, clingy silk, and the front of my gown had come open. I adjusted it, reddening.

"It's Mark's fault. He got me so worried about Spoodie, I didn't stop to put on any clothes. I didn't even brush my hair. I must look a fright."

Dave's smile told me I didn't. He kissed me and went home to sleep. I tumbled back into bed, and slept soundly until lunchtime.

fourteen

My shorthand course had finished. I enrolled for a typing course that would keep me at college until the end of Dave's final term. With tongue in cheek, I explained to my father that I was doing the course in order to be able to type out my university lecture notes.

"Of course," he agreed wryly, writing the check. "Here you are, then. My donation to the college. Mind you, honey, I'd be glad if you did actually manage to learn to type, despite that not being the main objective. Typing is a useful skill to have."

"I'll learn to type," I promised him. "Thanks, Dad."

He smiled abstractedly and began to sift through the pile of papers on his desk. He had brought home a lot of work from the office. I pocketed the check.

As I turned to go, he said suddenly, "Just so long as you're happy, Rhonnie."

"I'm happy," I told him.

I *was* happy. Dave and I were still seeing each other daily, and I was more in love than ever. Everything was fine; except that since the night of the party, I was aware of a constraint in Dave whenever we kissed or cuddled. It was nothing obvious, but I would sense him stiffen slightly, and he never allowed our embraces to last long enough to satisfy my own increased craving to be physically close to him. One evening, after he had given me an almost brotherly good-night kiss, I felt driven to ask what was wrong.

"Wrong? Nothing. Why?"

"Well, that wasn't much of a kiss. Can I have another?"

"Don't be greedy. Isn't one enough?"

"No," I said, locking my arms round his middle. "I won't let you go until you kiss me properly."

He laughed. "What's got into you all of a sudden?"

What had got into me wasn't that sudden. For days I had been trying to block out erotic thoughts about him. But now the actual feel of his body in close contact with mine was proving too much for my self-control. I put my face up to kiss him. He jerked his head back out of reach.

"Cut it out, will you?"

I dropped my arms. My cheeks felt stinging hot, as if they had been slapped hard.

He said, "I don't understand you. What do you want from me? I've told you I love you. Isn't that enough?"

"If you love somebody," I said in a dull resigned voice, "you like to be close to them. You like kissing them.

131

I'm not certain you do love me. I think you've gone off me."

He laughed, angrily this time. "Oh Christ! I can't win, can I? If I touch you, I get into trouble. If I keep my hands to myself, I get into trouble. Listen, do me a favor. Make up your mind, huh?"

His anger didn't strike me as real. I gave him a hurt smile. "I have made up my mind, Dave."

"Hell!" he said.

He sounded desperate. His face in the moonlight was silver tinted and surrealistic. I couldn't help myself; I had to caress him. With the tips of two fingers, I stroked a line down his forehead, his nose, over his mouth. The sensual pout of his underlip stretched into a smile.

"Please!" he muttered.

"Please?"

"Cut it out." He seized my shoulders and pushed me away. "Do you realize I'm writing exams in a month's time?"

"So?" I asked.

"So . . . I can't afford any . . . complications in my life right now."

I flinched. "Is that what I am to you? A complication?"

"I didn't say that."

"Then what are you trying to say? You—"

"I just think we shouldn't rush things." He made an irritable gesture. "All right?"

"All right," I heard myself say.

He hesitated before kissing me on the cheek. " 'Night then. Sleep well. See you tomorrow?"

"Yes," I said mechanically.

The hot, sunny weather continued. It was the start of a year of terrible drought, but we weren't to know that at the time. It was too soon in the season to be concerned over the lack of rain. Not that my thoughts dwelled much on the weather, anyway; in October, I had other things on my mind.

Near the middle of the month, Wendy's mother rang me. She was rather cagey on the telephone about what she wanted. But from the little she said, I gathered that Wendy wasn't well and her mother would like me to visit her. It was a Saturday morning. I drove straight over to their house in the Peugeot.

Mrs. Forest was waiting for me on the front porch. She led me into the living room and closed the door.

"Will you have a cup of tea, Rhonda?"

"No, thanks," I said. "But where's Wendy? Is she in bed?"

"At the moment, yes. She hasn't been well enough to go to university for a few days. Are you sure you won't have tea? Perhaps you'd prefer coffee?"

"No, really." I smiled tensely past her.

I never felt at ease with Wendy's mother; I had always found her a little forbidding and also totally lacking in a sense of humor. I began edging towards the door. She stepped in front of me.

"Rhonda, I'm very worried about Wendy. That's why

133

I rang you. I can't find out what the matter is with her. She won't talk to me, and she won't let me get a doctor. I'm hoping you'll . . . well, you are such an old friend, I'm sure she will confide in you."

I retreated. "We're not that close any longer, Mrs. Forest." My hand reached for the door. She grasped my other arm.

"It's that awful boy, Simon, Rhonda. I'm convinced he's to blame for all this. You know, Wendy hasn't been the same since she started going out with him. I've always suspected him of taking drugs; in fact, I'm certain he does, from the look of him. That's been a terrible worry to me. Now I'm so afraid he's . . . I'm afraid Wendy's got herself into . . . she isn't well at all, Rhonda. She ought to see a doctor. She won't listen to me, though. Perhaps you can persuade her?"

"I'll try. I'll talk to her." I felt briefly sorry for Mrs. Forest, but I wouldn't meet her eye; my first loyalty was to Wendy, and I meant her to know it. I opened the door.

"Rhonda? . . . You won't tell her I asked you to—"

"No, I won't tell her," I said, and made my escape.

Wendy was lying in bed with a sheet over her, listening to the radio. I wasn't prepared for how ill she looked. She was the color of a corpse. As I approached, she turned her head listlessly on the pillow.

"Oh, it's you," she said. "What are you doing here?"

"I've come to visit you. Are you up to having—hang on, let me help you." She was struggling to sit up.

"I can manage. I'm all right. I'm only tired."

While she reorganized her pillows and switched off the radio, I lowered myself onto the edge of the mattress and

134

examined her with concern. She was a spectral shadow of her former gaudy projection. Her hair had reverted to its natural mouse brown, and the innumerable narrow plaits hung limply round her face. There wasn't a trace of orange left in her appearance—the sun appeared to have suffered an eclipse. I cracked a joke about it, to try and raise a smile from her.

The joke fell flat. Her eyes confronted mine with a coldness bordering on animosity. "My mother asked you to come and visit me, didn't she?"

"No—what makes you think—I happened to be passing, and decided to drop in because I haven't seen you for ages."

"Bloody liar. I heard my mother ring you."

She turned her face away towards the window. Her eyes were red, the lids inflamed, as if she had been crying. I remembered all the hours she and I had spent in this room, on the bed, talking about our hopes for the future, our fears, our frustrations. A sudden despondency closed in on me.

I said, "Okay. I admit it. Your mother rang me. She's worried about you."

"I know," and she gave a hiccup of laughter. "She thinks I'm pregnant. But I'm not." She was watching me now. "I've had an abortion."

"God, Wendy! I—"

"God Wendy what?" There was venom in her tone.

"I wish you'd told me," I said lamely. "Maybe I could have helped."

"Helped? How could you have helped me? Do you know any doctors who are prepared to defy the law?"

"No, sorry, I—"

"Well, exactly. They're not easy to come by. That's why I had such a rough time—because it was left rather late. But at least the guy was qualified and knew what he was doing."

"Who was he? How did you manage to find—"

"It's not important . . . now." Closing her eyes, she leaned back on the wall. "If you tell my mother, I'll kill you," she said.

"As if I'd do that. But what about Simon? Did . . . I hope he—"

"Simon? Who's Simon?" She opened her left eye and smiled bleakly at me. "You mean . . . *Simon*. Ya, he helped. He found the abortionist."

"Has he been to see you?"

"What for? He wouldn't want to see me. We've split up. I'm not black enough to suit him. He's only really into Black women. The blacker the better." Her lower lip curled in a sardonic leer. "And he thinks he's unconditioned and liberated. He thinks *he's* not color conscious. Jeez!" She banged her head against the wall. "I'm sick of it—we're all so screwed up in this crappy country."

I refused to accept that. "We aren't all," I retorted. "But Simon obviously is. If you ask me, Wend, you're well rid of him."

"You think you aren't screwed up?" She focused on me; there was contempt in her gaze, and sarcastic amusement. "You think you look at Black people as people?"

"As people? Of course I do."

"You look at a Black guy the same way you look at a White guy?"

136

I resented the question, and its inference, and the cynical smirk on her face. Forcing a laugh, I said, "I should jolly well hope not. I'm not kinky like Simon."

"No, you're horribly so-called normal," she said sardonically. "A classic case of successful conditioning."

That did it. Scooping up my bag, I rose to go, groping in my pocket for the car keys.

"By the way, Rhonda, who is the bloke with the motorbike?" she asked then.

The keys weren't in my pocket. I searched my bag. "Which bloke are you talking about?"

"I saw you the other day, zooming along Oxford Road. He looked quite juicy. Who is he? Anyone special?"

"Damnation!" I said. "Where are they?"

"Are you hunting for your keys? They're here." She held them up; I grabbed them from her. "Before you leave, Rhond, you couldn't spare me a smoke, could you? I've run out."

"Help yourself." With ill grace, I flung the packet on the bed and walked across the room.

On the easel in the corner stood an unfinished painting. It was a portrait—a self-portrait. The identity of the face was immediately recognizable, despite its consisting as yet of only the eyes, nostrils, and mouth. The mouth was twisted open, the teeth bared in a cry of pain that was savagely exaggerated by the absence of any peripheral margin to the face. Above the two bullet-hole nostrils, Wendy's cobalt-blue eyes stared out dully, the pupils contracted to black pinpoints, the irises flat and filmy. I was being shown Wendy as I had never perceived her before.

I recrossed the room, sank down on the bed, and lit a

cigarette. The smoke scorched my throat. My fingers felt for Wendy's hand.

"You've had one helluva time, old girl. I'm sorry," I said inadequately.

She shrugged. "Tell me about the bloke with the bike. I'm still waiting. What's the big secret? Don't you trust me? I won't try to pinch him from you, I promise."

"You'd better not!" I said, smiling.

"It's like that, is it?"

"It is."

"So? Who is he?"

"His name's Dave."

"That tells me a whole lot."

"What else do you want me to tell you?"

"How long have you been involved with him?"

"Since August."

"Oh wow! . . . That's got to be a record for you. It must be serious."

"It's very serious." I directed my gaze at the glowworm end of her cigarette. "As far as I'm concerned."

The worm dropped off onto the bodice of her satin dressing gown. She brushed it away with her thumb, leaving a smudge of ash across the embroidery of red hearts. "You're not certain about *him*?"

"Ya . . . I am."

"You sound it," she said.

I picked up a stub out of the ashtray and squeezed the cotton-wool filter between my nails. "Ag, I don't know . . . it's just . . ." I let the stub fall back in the ashtray.

"You think he's only after your body?"

138

"He isn't. That's the problem," I finally admitted. "I want our relationship to be physical. He doesn't. Or rather, he says he doesn't want us to rush things. Still . . . " Putting on a smile, I heaved myself up off the bed. "Possibly he's right, and I should count my blessings; at least I don't have to worry about falling pregnant, do I?"

"You needn't worry on that score. I wasn't on the pill, you know. And a couple of times when I was doped up to my eyeballs, I forgot to take any precautions at all." She regarded me impassively as I straightened my clothes. "Stupid of me. Not so?"

"Very." I bent to kiss her good-bye.

"Thanks for coming," she said. "And good luck with your bloke. What are you going to do about him?"

"Nothing. What can I do?"

"Use your charms. Seduce him."

"I can't," I told her tersely.

"Have you tried?"

"*Tried?* When I hug him, he practically freezes up."

She made no comment and settled her head back tiredly on the pillow. I gave her my packet of Dunhill and asked if there was anything else I could do. She shook her head.

"Look after yourself," I said. " 'Bye, Wend."

" 'Bye."

I was on my way to the door when she called my name. I pivoted round. "Yes?"

She said, "Perhaps he's queer."

"What . . . ?" Blood rushed to my face. "Oh rubbish! Of course he isn't, Wendy. Honestly! You—just because you hang around with perverts, you believe everybody is. There's nothing wrong with Dave."

139

She was propped up on her elbows, her plaits dangling and twisted like snakes. "Queers, you know, Rhonda, are also people," she said, and rolled over on her side, presenting her back.

I left. To avoid Mrs. Forest, I slipped out of the house through the kitchen.

fifteen

A week later, Lynn rang me. I hadn't seen or heard from her since she had dropped out of the shorthand course.

"How's Dave?" she asked at once.

"He's here," I told her. "Would you like to speak to him?"

She gave a whoop down the line. "Mazel tov! So the two of you have got it together?"

"Got what together?" I said a bit peevishly, and was subjected to a dirty chuckle.

"Never mind. Hey, look, Rhond, why don't you bring him over? I'm at Joel's. We're sort of celebrating, and there are some people I—"

"Joel? Joel who?"

"He's—hang on." I heard her talking to someone. There

was the sound of laughter in the background. "Rhond? Sorry, that was Joel. He says I must tell you he's very nice, but he isn't. He's a lousy *schmuck*, really. Listen, Rh— Hey, stop that! Joel! Take your—" From the noises being made, I surmised that he was doing something to her that she was enjoying. Resentfully I waited. Eventually, a mellow male voice said, "Rhonda, this is Joel speaking. How are you?"

"I'm all right," I said curtly. "How are you?"

"Come and join the party. You know where I live?" He told me the address. I wrote it down. Then he handed the receiver back to Lynn.

"You coming, Rhond?" she asked.

"I don't think so," I said.

I wasn't in the mood for a party—especially one where I expected to find couples draped all over each other. I didn't feel I could handle such a situation with things the way they were between Dave and me. But I was loath to explain that to Lynn.

"You must come," she insisted. "I haven't seen you for ages."

"All right," I grudgingly agreed. "If Dave wants to come, we'll come."

"Tell him he'd better. I won't forgive him if you don't show up. And bring your swimming things."

The family were having afternoon tea on the patio. My father was half asleep in his chair. Victor was reading the Sunday newspapers. Helen and my mother were talking about funerals. Dave and Mark were sitting apart from the others, at the far edge of the patio, cleaning Mark's pellet gun. Dave had removed his shirt. He was built like

142

a sprinter: lean and lithe with compact muscles. Weeks of daily exposure to the sun had burned his body to a rich bronze.

I went up behind him and leaned my hands on his shoulders. He was explaining to Mark how the trigger mechanism worked, and took no notice of me. Rubbing myself against his back, I kneaded my fingers into his flesh. He shook me off.

"Don't jolt me, I'm pouring oil," he muttered.

"Go 'way," Mark told me. "Can't you see me and Dave are busy? Boy-oh-boy! Girls!" he said to Dave. "I don't know why you *smaak* 'em."

"He doesn't," I snapped impetuously.

Dave's spine stiffened. I noticed that under the brim of my father's hat, one eye was half open and swiveled in our direction. Screening my face with my hair, I glared at the back of Dave's head.

"Lynn's invited us to a party," I said grumpily.

"When?" he mumbled.

"Now. Do you want to go?"

"I'm game," he said.

"Hurry up, then." And I flounced into the house to fetch the address.

We got lost several times en route to Joel's house. I was sulking and communicated only in monosyllables. Dave withdrew into a sullen silence. My earlier accusation festered between us like an untreated splinter.

Lynn met us at the door and ushered us into the kitchen, where she was preparing sandwiches. Joel appeared. I felt instantly drawn to him. He was thin and dark, and he had a friendly, direct manner and an engaging grin that crin-

143

kled up his face. Both he and Lynn were a little tipsy. I was thankful that they were too wrapped up in each other to notice the atmosphere between Dave and me.

Joel took us into the garden to join the other guests, who were enjoying themselves round the swimming pool. He poured us drinks, then excused himself and returned inside. I started making polite conversation with the nearest girl. At some point I realized Dave was no longer beside me. Looking around, I finally spotted him at the opposite end of the pool. He was kneeling on the grass, chatting to someone—a blond, handsome hulk of a guy in a swimsuit. A *handsome hulk* . . . My hand lurched, slopping most of the gin-and-tonic out of my glass. I smiled apologetically at the girl and retreated, staring across the pool.

It wasn't a trick of the imagination; he definitely was *the* Handsome Hulk.

I decided I needed a refill. I topped up my glass at the drinks table. Then, apprehensively, I walked across the lawn.

"Hi," I said to Dave. "I was wondering where you had vanished to."

The Handsome Hulk stood up to be introduced. He towered above me. He was even bigger and more beautiful than I had remembered him to be. His name sounded beautiful to me too: Bruce—it suited him. He folded his towel for me to sit on and squatted on the grass. Dave immediately picked up their two empty glasses.

"I'll get you another beer," he told Bruce and left us alone together.

The sun was shining in my eyes. I shielded them with

144

my hands and squinted at Bruce from under my palms. He was squinting at me.

"You know, I'm sure we've seen each other before," I said.

"We have? Where?"

I told him.

"I'm sorry, I don't remember," he said. "I do sometimes go to the college because a friend of mine lectures there; and I've had coffee in the canteen with him once or twice. But I'm afraid I can't recall ever seeing—"

"Not that it's important," I hurriedly interrupted him.

He turned his ultramarine eyes full on me. Their brilliant blueness, overhung by a thick lock of golden blond hair, had a dazzling impact. I sought refuge in my glass; the mouthful of gin tasted like champagne. I felt intoxicated and irresponsible.

"So how come you know Dave?" I blurted out.

"I don't, really. I only met him last Saturday when I took one of my motorbikes to him to be repaired. He did a terrific job on it too. I've just been telling him I want him to keep all my bikes tuned up for me in future."

"*All* your bikes? How many are there?"

"Three," he said, and grinned. "Do you think that's greedy?"

"Yes. You can't need three, surely?"

"I do. I race them, you see, and I keep crashing."

The amused directness of his gaze flustered me. "You—you race motorbikes? As a hobby?"

"It isn't a hobby, exactly. It's more like a way of life."

"I'd call it a way of death," I said, and was flattered by his laughter. "Especially if you keep crashing."

145

"I try not to."

"Perhaps I could come and watch you race one day," I ventured boldly.

"Sure. Anytime. Get Dave to bring you."

Dave. I had managed to put him out of my mind for the moment. But now I saw him approaching. Lynn and Joel were with him, and several others whom I didn't know. They all joined us. Lynn was chatting to Dave; he handed Bruce his beer and sat down next to her.

We had become a noisy group. I didn't have a chance to say anything further to Bruce. Joel was talking to him. I tried to eavesdrop on their conversation. I heard enough to learn that they were both undergraduates at Wits and actively involved in student politics. From what Joel was saying, I gathered he was heavily committed to the fight against Apartheid. After a bit, I felt bored by their discussion and stopped listening.

More and more people were joining our circle. A leering, toothy Lothario, clutching a vodka bottle, made drunken advances to me. I lit a cigarette and blew smoke in his face, whereupon he offered himself to the plump girl who had spread herself at my feet. He had more luck there. She was decidedly the worse for wear and welcomed him with open arms.

I stared at Bruce, hoping to attract his attention. He looked round once, and smiled; but not at me. I turned. He was smiling at Dave. A wink passed between them. Then Dave's gaze intercepted mine.

Our eyes locked. His held an appeal that sent a thrill of pain through me. But I cut him dead and looked away.

The inevitable happened next. Someone started telling

146

blue jokes. They were neither very original nor funny; everybody laughed uproariously, nevertheless. Lothario was then inspired to recount his supply of jokes, all of which began, "Did you hear about the queer who—"

I was afraid to glance at Dave for fear of what might be showing in his face. Egged on by a few members of the group, Lothario—who evidently considered himself to be a great comedian—was putting on a performance as an effeminate homosexual.

"I'm a nithe boy, really," he assured us all in a squeaky falsetto. Clutching onto the plump girl for support, he swayed to his knees and wriggled his hips suggestively, fluttering his eyelashes at the closest male. "Don't you think tho, dahling? I can'th help being a panthy. Oooo, you are secthy. Would you like to see my petals?" He pulled down the back of his swimming trunks. The plump girl yanked them up again smartly, amid general laughter.

Abruptly, a figure rose from the grass. The sudden movement took the lot of us by surprise. Heads jerked round like a startled flock of sheep. The sun had slid lower down the sky; Bruce's tall form blotted it out. From my angle of vision, he was a beautiful, blazing gold silhouette before he moved forward. He walked over to stand in front of Lothario. There was nothing menacing in his manner and yet the rest of us were tensely silent, as if we could sense something dramatic was about to occur. His hands came up from his sides, and Lothario's face showed fear. Folding his arms across his chest, Bruce grinned down at him.

"We aren't all pansies," he informed him pleasantly, "us *queers*, as you like to call us. And in case you're getting

147

any wrong ideas right now, I can assure you that I'm *very* particular about whom I fancy. So *you* needn't worry; you've nothing to fear from me."

"I'm . . . not . . . afraid of you," Lothario blustered.

"No." Bruce eyed him pityingly. "It's yourself you're afraid of, I reckon." And he stepped over him and walked on towards the house, calling back, " 'Bye Joel, thanks for the party."

Joel sprang up and went after him; Lynn let out an expletive and followed. She was followed by Dave. He stood up and strode straight past me as if I weren't there. Nobody else twitched a muscle until the four of them had disappeared through the door into the kitchen. Then, like a delayed shock wave after an explosion, there was a tumult of embarrassed reaction from the group.

The girl next to me tugged at my arm. "I don't believe it. Do you believe it? Bruce—queer? He can't be. He's so gorgeous. Don't you think he's gorgeous? I think he's divine. Jeez! It's not fair. What a waste! You know, I—"

"Excuse me," I said. I prized her fingers off my wrist, pushed myself up, and stumbled out of the circle.

At the kitchen door, I hesitated. The room appeared to be empty. I went in. Dave was leaning against the side of the refrigerator, drinking a glass of milk. His eyes glanced off mine.

He said, "I'm ready to go. Do you want to stay?"

"What for?" I retorted. "I'm not enjoying myself. Where's Lynn?"

"She and Joel are seeing Bruce off at the gate. They'll be back in a minute."

"I must say good-bye to her. We'd better wait."

Lynn, when she returned, tried to dissuade us from leaving. Dave told her he had to go home and study. I insisted that I had things to do. After giving each of us a sharp look, she let us depart, with a plea to me to ring her soon. None of us mentioned Bruce, or referred to what had just happened out in the garden.

As Dave and I walked to his bike, he said in a constricted, polite voice, "Nice house, isn't it? Joel's parents are away, so they have it all to themselves for a week."

"Who has?" I asked crossly.

"Joel and Lynn. Who else?"

"Well, bully for them."

My acid tone put a stop to any further conversation. He dropped me off at our front gate. I didn't invite him in.

" 'Bye," I said. "Thanks for the lift." I began moving away.

"Rhonda? . . . Hang on! *Rhonda!*"

I walked back slowly. "What do you want?"

He spoke a few words that were inaudible.

"I can't hear you," I said, not very civilly, and he cut the engine.

"Rhonda . . . look, this isn't going to work, is it? Us, I mean."

I should have known that was what he would say. I had been telling myself much the same thing all afternoon. But hearing *him* say it was another matter. A feeling of dread rose from the pit of my stomach. I frowned fiercely at the spot in the road where J.R. had been run over; it had remained a slightly darker color than the surrounding area.

Swallowing painfully, I said, "Why don't you come out with it?"

When he failed to answer, I stared up. He was gazing mutely into my face. His eyes seemed to be asking me for help. I was suddenly certain I was right about him.

"It's okay," I choked out. "You needn't bother to tell me. I already know."

"Know what?"

He had been put on his guard. He looked guilty to me now, and defensive. Jealousy clawed at me.

"You like Bruce, don't you?" I threw at him.

My words produced no response. He said nothing, did nothing. For a mortifyingly long time he just sat there on the bike, contemplating me with a hard, penetrating stare, as if he was probing for something that might help him answer. Eventually, he gave a start, and shook his head. A small, bitter smile stiffened his mouth.

"I admire him. He's got a helluva lot of guts," he said.

The strength of feeling behind his words was like a red rag to a wounded bull. I couldn't contain myself any longer. "Ya, *he* has. At least he has the guts to be honest about himself. At least he doesn't try to pass himself off as something he isn't. Well, he obviously fancies you too, so you're—"

"Fancies me? You think he—hey, what makes you think I fancy him?"

"Oh, come off it! I might be stupid, but I'm not blind. I saw the way you were looking at each other."

"You did?" He laughed his painful laugh. "So you're telling me I'm queer."

150

"Aren't you?" I said, sneering to disguise the trembling of my bottom lip.

"And if I am? If I were to admit that I'm . . . gay— what then?"

"What then?" I threw my hands up. "My God! Doesn't it even bother you that you've been taking me for a ride? Telling me that you *love* me and all that rubbish! Christ, I must be really stupid. How could I be so gullible, when it's so obvious now. I never turned you on, did I? It was all make-believe for you, while I . . . For bloody weeks I've been torturing myself thinking I must have some how put you off me physically, that it was my fault you . . . you . . ." I had to stop; my voice was out of control. Dave's face dissolved into a fuzzy blob in front of me.

He stamped on the starter pedal. The engine thundered. His face swam closer. His lips moved.

"Thank you," he whispered hoarsely.

"For what?" I yelped.

"You've just proved to me how understanding you are."

The bike flashed past and diminished in a hazy blur. I knew he had gone, this time, for good. Tears were stream-ing down my cheeks, but I believed I was glad to be rid of him.

sixteen

I felt angry and bitter for a whole day and two nights. I had completed my typing course the previous week, so I had no reason to leave the house—not that I would have gone to college, anyway. I told my mother I had a migraine and stayed in my room, wishing fervently that I could board the first plane to London.

On Tuesday morning I woke up with a sense of remorse and spent the day fighting with myself. On Wednesday I rushed around, madly doing things to keep busy. On Thursday I couldn't make myself do anything. It was an insufferably long day; I constantly looked at my watch and wondered what Dave was doing and how he was. By the end of Friday afternoon, I felt desolate.

I had never rung Dave before—there had been no need to when I was seeing him daily. But he had given me his number at the start of our relationship. I looked it up in my address book and used the telephone in my father's study. I didn't want my mother or Mark listening in.

The ringing tone went on and on. With each ring, my heart beat ten times faster. A voice said, "Hallo." Dave's voice.

My tongue was stuck to the roof of my mouth. "Dave?" I heard him take a sharp breath. "D-Dave, yes, it's m-me," I stuttered. "I'm just . . . I want to say I'm . . . I'm sorry I was—I wasn't very understanding on Sunday. But I didn't mean . . . well, I hope we can still be friends."

"Why?" he asked gruffly.

"Because I miss you. . . . H-how are you?"

"Couldn't be better. I write my first exam on Monday, I'm supposed to be studying, and I can't get a bleeding thing into my head."

"I'm sorry—have I disturbed you?"

The telephone seemed to magnify the pain in his laugh. "You always have," he said. Then he muttered a few words that sounded like "If only you knew—" and rang off.

If only I knew? Knew *what*? I redialed his number. The line was engaged. I tried again, half a dozen times, and decided he must have taken the receiver off the hook.

Behind me, the door burst open and Mark charged in. He was dressed up in his Cub's uniform.

"I've been looking E-V-E-R-Y-W-H-E-R-E for you," he complained. "Mom says I've got to tell you she's gone

153

to meet Dad at work and they're going to pick up some guy from the airport and take him out to dinner and they'll be home very late and you've got to fix your own dinner because Sophie's been given the evening off and you must feed Spoodie and if you go out you must take a key and . . ." He had run out of breath and was gulping like a fish.

"I'm not going out, so relax! You'll suffocate yourself one day if you're not careful."

"I bet you'd be glad. Is Dave coming tonight? If he is, don't forget to ask him for me if he—"

"Are you stone-deaf? How many times do I have to tell you that Dave is writing exams. I *won't* be seeing him."

"So what if he's writing exams? He's clever, like me. He doesn't need to study. You know what I think? I think you aren't seeing him because you've had a row. And that's why you're such an old crosspatch."

"GOOD-BYE, Mark."

He doffed his cap mockingly. "You'll be sorry, 'cause I'm not coming home tonight. You'll be all alone. I'm staying over at Micky's after Cubs. Mom said I could. So you'll—"

"And Spoodie? Who's meant to look after her? Where will she sleep?"

"She can sleep in your bedroom. I don't mind, if it's only for one night. But if a burglar breaks in, you mustn't let him steal her, you hear?"

"Steal *her*? What about *me*?"

"A burglar wouldn't want you," he said, snickering. "Man, I've got to fly. Micky's mother is picking me up at the gate."

154

The front door slammed after him. Ten seconds later, the bell rang.

"It's a burglar," Mark said as I opened the door.

"What do you want? Have you forgotten something?"

He rubbed his ankle against the calf of his other leg, twisting his cap in his hands. His face had a shifty look.

"Don't you *smaak* Dave?" he asked me.

"Of course I— Why do you—"

"You shouldn't fight with him, Rhond. He's a *lekker**
guy. I *smaak* him. Lots. I wouldn't mind if you married him. True's bob!" he said, and having embarrassed himself, turned tail and scuttled off the front step.

I fed Spoodie on the patio and sat out there, watching the sunset. The sky in the west looked like a bleeding wound. I thought I understood why people started drinking at sundown.

When I heard Dave's bike, I refused to let myself believe it was him until I actually saw him walking up the drive. As I ran to meet him, he stopped and raised his hands in the air.

"I give up. I'm sick of trying to concentrate. I *can't*. I'll just have to fail."

"You won't fail, Dave. That's nonsense," I told him. "You'll pass with flying colors. You'll see. I know you will. You're much too clever to fail."

His eyes scanned what I was wearing: a V-necked, embroidered T-shirt and skimpy shorts. "You aren't going out this evening?" he asked.

---

*terrific

"Dressed like this? You've got to be kidding. Hey!" Impulsively, I gripped his hand. "Come and have a nice cold beer. That'll make you feel better."

I poured him a lager and opened a big packet of crisps. Spoodie brought him a dog biscuit, then growled when he tried to take it from her. Dave dropped down on all fours and growled back, and they had a game, chasing each other through the living room and round the patio. I laughed at them both, ready to burst from the pressure of unexpected, sudden happiness.

The wound in the sky had healed; the west was now suffused with a lambent rosiness, like a fireside glow after the blaze has died down. I shifted my chair to face in that direction. Dave picked up his glass from the table and came to stand at my shoulder.

"Isn't it a beautiful color?" I murmured.

"It is."

I glanced at him out of the side of my eye. He wasn't sharing the sunset with me. His gaze was concentrated on the back of my head. I felt the ticklish touch of his fingers as they combed down through my hair.

"Veld grass," he said in a tremulous undertone. "It *is* like veld grass. In the dawn."

I gave an unsteady laugh. "Dawn?"

"Poetic license. Where are your folks this evening?"

"They've gone out to dinner."

"Mark too?"

"No, he's spending the night at Micky's house."

"When will your parents be back?"

"Very late, I imagine. Why?"

"Just checking."

156

He wandered over to Spoodie, who was pursuing her tail in senseless, giddy circles. Seizing the wispy appendage, he offered her the tip, but she went for his hand instead. He fended her off while he drank his beer. Then he grinned across at me.

"I'm not gay, you know," he said, and he put his glass down and started wrestling with Spoodie.

"What did you . . . Dave? . . . Dave!"

He probably couldn't hear me; the pair of them were making a lot of noise. I retrieved his glass, which was in danger of being broken, and shot into the house. I rushed to my bedroom and surveyed my face in the mirror. It was flushed and glowing. My hair was mussed up. Working at feverish speed, I brushed out the tangles, dabbed on a touch of lipstick to match the color of my cheeks, sprinkled some scent behind my ears, and sprinted down the passage.

In the liquor cabinet was an opened bottle of sherry. I grabbed it and a glass, snatched a beer from the refrigerator, and darted into the hall to check my face once more in the mirror hanging there. *Now slow down,* I warned myself. *Don't start expecting too much. Probably nothing is going to happen. Just remember, all that matters is that he's come back. He's here. That's all that matters.*

The light was already fading outside, and at first glance, the patio appeared to be empty. My heart gave a sickening lurch. In a hoarse, fear-filled whisper, I spoke his name and he answered from behind me. He was lying full-length on one of the rubber rafts, which were normally kept stacked up against the wall when not in use in the swimming pool.

"I'm recovering from being mauled by Spoodie," he said. "I had to find her something else to chew instead of me. . . . What have you got there?"

"Sherry for me, and another beer for you."

He pushed himself up into a sitting position and took the drinks from me.

"Where am I supposed to sit?" I asked. He patted the raft. "It's too close to the ground," I objected. "Corn crickets might—"

"Never mind them. They don't bite you like these ruddy mosquitoes." He slapped at the air in front of his face, then reached for my arm and pulled me down beside him. "That's better. Now they can bite you, rather than me."

"Thanks a lot. Now I know how much you care for me," I told him.

He unscrewed the cap of the sherry bottle, filled my glass, and handed it to me.

"You don't."

He had spoken very quietly, almost under his breath. But his voice was charged with a current of emotion that electrified every cell in my body. He leaned back with his beer, bringing his shoulder against mine. The warm pressure of the contact sent a radiant heat down the whole of my left side.

I needed both hands to steady my glass, and I was glad of the darkness as I asked, "How *do* you feel about me, Dave?"

The raft sagged and bulged up again. He had shifted and was digging in his pocket. An arm came forward; his fingers brushed my throat, and the weight of the locket lifted off my neck. The clasp clicked open. Instinctively, I seized his wrist.

"Hey, don't—Dave, you're not taking your shell back?"

"I'm answering your question." He put down his beer and my glass. "Give me your hand," he said. "Open it."

The hard, rounded coldness of the cowrie pressed into my palm; he closed my hand over it into a tight fist. I realized then that I was holding two cowries, fitted together, mouth to mouth, one on top of the other.

I shut my eyes, smiling. His arms enclosed me. Blindly, hearing only the thudding of my own heartbeat, I offered my face up to his.

He was very gentle. He began with teasing kisses. When he tugged my T-shirt out of my shorts and slid it up over my head, his hands were shaking. As he fumbled at the catch on my bra, a sudden alarm bell rang in my mind. I tore my mouth from his.

"Dave, we can't—we mustn't go the whole way. I'm not on the pill. I might fall preg—"

"No, you won't. Don't worry." He kissed my earlobe. "I've taken care of it."

"You have? How—"

"I brought something with me, and while you were in the house I—no, sshh! Please! Don't talk, just help me undo this damn thing—I can't wait much longer."

His urgency communicated itself to me. I groped at my back with fingers nearly as clumsy as his. The straps slipped down my arms and I heard him draw in his breath. Next moment I was flat on my back on the raft, and he was half on top of me, struggling to get my shorts off. I tore at the buttons on his shirt, desperate to feel his body naked against mine.

"Don't!" He quivered. "Don't touch me." He sat up abruptly. "Damn! Oh hell . . . !"

"What's happened?" I gasped. "What did I do?"

"I'm too damn close to the brink. I need to cool down a bit. Maybe I ought to jump in the pool."

He made as if to stand up. But there was no way I was going to allow him to leave me in this state, even briefly. I pulled him back down on top of me. My shorts and pants were caught round my ankles. I kicked them free and frantically helped him peel off his own clothes.

Our mouths fused, our bare bodies came together. And then I felt a tearing pain as he entered me. I let out a small involuntary cry, which was immediately lost in his explosive release. He lay over me, shuddering and groaning into my ear.

"Rhonda . . . Oh Christ! . . . Rhonda . . . Rhonda!"

I held him until his body stilled and he was quiet. He lifted his face and rested his forehead on mine.

"I'm sorry," he breathed. "I hurt you, didn't I?"

"It doesn't matter," I said dully. My only feeling now was a numbing sense of disappointment.

He propped himself up on his elbows to look at me. I closed my eyes so that he couldn't see into them. His fingers smoothed a sticky strand of hair off my cheek.

"You know I didn't—I thought you . . . I never realized you were a virgin. Are you all right?"

"Fine," I mumbled.

He swore softly and buried his face in my hair. "God, I love you."

160

I tightened my arms round his back. His mouth was caressing my ear. With unhurried gentleness, he started to make love to me again. My desire reawakened under his stroking, exploring hand. His tongue and lips teased and tantalized. The little tingling currents of heat radiating through my body mounted into waves. I felt him stir and swell within me, and as we began to move in time together, pain blended into sharpening pulsations of pleasure. I clung to him, moaning, and wanting it to go on and on. When he came at last, it was too soon for me. But the spasms that shook his body made me cry out with him. And as the waves of exquisite sensation slowly subsided, I was left feeling peculiarly at peace and satisfied. At least for the time being.

Dave was quiet in my arms. I lay and listened to the sounds of the night around us: the faint distant barking of a dog; the strident chorus of crickets in the shrubbery bordering the patio; the sporadic burping croak of a frog; and nearer at hand, regular small whiffling snores from Spoodie, who was curled up where she wasn't supposed to be—on the most comfortable chair. Her black head was invisible in the dark, the rest of her discernible as a ghostly gray nimbus.

I raised my wrist and peered at my watch.

"What's the time?" Dave murmured.

"I can't see. No—don't move." I clutched him. "Not yet."

"Hadn't we better get dressed? Somebody might come."

"We'd hear a car. Besides, as there aren't any lights on, a visitor would assume nobody was at home and go away again."

"Your parents wouldn't. What do you think they'd do if they discovered us *in flagrante delicto*?"

"*In flagr*—" I laughed. "Well, you obviously shouldn't worry about passing your Latin."

"I'm not worried—now. I don't give a damn about anything anymore, except us."

I squeezed him possessively. "Dave?"

"Mmm?"

"This wasn't your first time, was it?"

"Mmm."

"Liar."

"It's true," he said, rubbing his cheek against mine, like a cat. "The other times don't count—because . . ." His lips brushed across my face. "I wasn't in love." And he kissed me very softly on the mouth.

His tenderness at that particular moment made me feel uniquely beautiful and desirable and content. I smiled up at him voluptuously. He grinned.

"Believe me?"

"Yes." I sighed. "Kiss me again."

"Enough's enough. My bum is freezing. I have to put on some clothes."

I got my wish, however, though it wasn't quite what I was expecting. As Dave moved, a small, furry projectile launched itself at me; and before I understood what was happening, I found myself being kissed energetically all over my face by a hairy muzzle and warm wet tongue.

"Help me," I appealed to Dave, but he just laughed.

"I was wondering when she would join in," he said, and headed for the bathroom with his clothes.

162

Spoodie slithered off the raft and chased after him. I dressed hurriedly and followed them indoors to switch on the lights and draw the curtains. There was some dinner left over from the night before. I warmed it up, and we ate off our laps, snuggled up to each other on the sofa in the living room. Dave went home soon afterwards. I walked with him down the driveway.

"Do you think you'll be able to study now?" I asked him as he hugged me in the shadow of the gatepost.

"No," he said. "And I hope you won't be able to sleep. I hope you have wet dreams about me."

I ran my fingers lovingly over the top of his head. His scalp was a bit bristly; but the bristles felt silky and soft, like the fine fuzz of hairs on a leaf. There was so much my hands had still to discover about his body; I didn't know how I would survive until I saw him again.

"Dave. My Dave, what are we going to do?"

"Do?"

"My parents don't go out together for the whole evening all that often, and Mark is nearly always here. We might not have another chance to be alone for weeks and weeks."

"I've been thinking that too. It's terrible, isn't it?"

"So what will we do?"

"We'll have to work out something."

"I already have," I then admitted.

"Great." He held me away so that he could look at me. "Go on, I'm all ears. Tell me."

"Not yet," I decided, having briefly considered the cost of my plan. It would be expensive, and Dave needed

163

whatever money he had saved for university. I said, "I'll tell you once I've arranged it. I'd like it to be my present to you for passing your exams."

"Does that mean I've got to wait until my results come out?"

"Good grief, no! That's much too long to wait. I'll take your word for it that you've passed, after you've written your last paper. I trust you—though I shouldn't, really."

"You shouldn't?"

I nudged him in the side. "No, I shouldn't. After all, you let me believe you were gay. That was mighty mean of you, Dave. Why did you do it?"

"I was testing you," he said.

One half of his face was palely illuminated by the street lamp, the other half blacked out by a deep shadow. In trying to fathom his expression, being unable to see both his eyes was even more disquieting than his answer had been.

"And now you're cross," he said. His arms caught me and held me fast. "I'm sorry. Don't be cross . . . *please!*"

"I'm not," I told him. "I'm hurt."

He crushed my body against his. I let him hold me briefly, then resisted, loosening his grasp.

"Just tell me one thing. Are you *still* test—"

"I need you!" His hands swept through my hair. "I need you. I can't give you up. You know, when you rang me today I—I . . . God! Rhonda, I love you. I love you *so much*."

The brutal force of his embrace knocked the breath out of my body. "Me too" was all I could gasp.

164

"We must be very careful, though. You mustn't fall pregnant."

"Heaven forbid! No! I'll make sure I'm on the pill before next time. Hell, Dave, if only you didn't have exams to write. When will I see you?"

"As soon as possible. I'll ring you tomorrow," he promised.

seventeen

I made the necessary reservations through a travel agent in town. Two return air tickets to Cape Town; and a fortnight in a luxurious hotel at Sea Point, in a double bedroom with private bathroom and a sea view. I didn't give a second thought to the expense because I knew I had more than enough money in the bank to pay for the holiday. Money wasn't the problem. The problem was what to tell my parents. Lynn, whom I visited on my way back from town, provided me with a plausible solution.

I went home and casually announced to my mother that I was going on holiday with Dave to Cape Town for two weeks, immediately after his exams were over. Before she had time to react, I explained that we would be staying with his relatives in Clifton, who had offered to put us up.

"Who are these people?" my mother asked suspiciously.

"Robert and Nancy Cohen. Nancy is Dave's cousin." In fact, she was Lynn's cousin. "They sound very nice. They're a married couple with two small children. And their flat is practically on the seafront so we'll—"

"Flat?" My mother's eyebrows rose. "If they've got a flat, not a house, and *two* children, they can't have much spare space. Where will you sleep?"

My answer came glibly, having been rehearsed beforehand. "In one of the kids' bedrooms. Dave will sleep on a camp bed in the living room. It will be a bit of a squash, but we don't mind. We'll only be there in the evening. We want to spend all day on the beach if the weather is good."

"And how do you propose getting down to Cape Town? Not on Dave's motor—"

"We'll be flying down. I've already booked our seats on the plane."

She straightened her posture and closed the nursery seed catalogue on her lap. "I presume, then, you've spoken to your father about it," she said in a brittle voice.

"I haven't. I didn't think there was any need to. I'm paying for the holiday out of my own money, so I fail to see why either of you should have any objections."

"Do you, indeed?"

"Hey, Mom, come on," I rallied her. "I reckon I'm old enough now to take responsibility for my own actions."

"You may think you are." She managed to rise from the armchair without bending her back, and automatically turned to smooth out the cushion. "We'll have to find out what your father feels about it. I suppose we *can* trust you to behave in a morally responsible manner."

"By which you mean?" I asked, only after she had walked away and couldn't see my suddenly red face.

She clattered out of the room on her high heels, leaving my question unanswered.

I was expecting a call from Dave in a little while. He had been ringing me every day at more or less the same time. I made a cup of coffee, shut myself in my father's study, and stared at the receiver, willing it to ring. It did, eventually.

"Were you sitting at the phone?" he asked.

"Dave . . . I'm missing you awfully," I croaked. "Are you—how did the history exam go?"

"It went," he said cryptically. "That's two down, four more to tackle, and then . . ."

"Yes? And then?"

"I was wondering . . . perhaps we could go off on holiday somewhere for a couple of weeks?"

I smiled to myself. "Great minds think alike. How does the idea of two weeks at the sea grab you, Dave?"

"It grabs me. I'll find out about hotel prices in Durban. If they're too expensive, we'll camp. I've got a small tent we can strap on the bike."

"Nothing doing," I said. "We're not camping. We're staying in a four-star hotel on the seafront, and we're traveling there and back in comfort—we're flying. It has all been arranged. And there's nothing to pay. That's been taken care of as well."

"Who by?" he asked guardedly.

"Me. It's the present I promised—now, please, Dave,

you mustn't give me a hard time," I pleaded as he tried to butt in. "I don't need my money for university like you do. Anyway, if we love each other, what difference does it make who pays?"

"It does to me," he said emphatically.

I sighed. "I was afraid you might be difficult. Quit being such a male chauvinist. If you had more money than me, I wouldn't object to you standing me a holiday . . . Dave . . . ?"

"I'll pay for the hotel."

"If you love me, you'll accept my present," I stubbornly insisted.

A rustle and a small scratching sound, like a mouse in a cupboard, came from his end of the line. I gathered he was lighting a cigarette.

I gave him a few seconds to grapple with his male ego; then I said cajolingly, "Of course, I do expect you to pay me back in kind; I'm looking forward to that. Also, I hope you'll take me to the top of Table Mountain by cableway because—"

"Table Mountain? What are you talking about? Table Mountain is in Cape Town, not Durban."

"Ya, I know. I'm talking about Cape Town. That's where I've booked the holiday. I thought it would be more romantic than Durban." As an afterthought, I asked, "You don't mind, do you? The Cape is so beautiful."

He exhaled audibly and said nothing. I was rapidly running out of patience with what I considered to be his stupid masculine pride. Resentfully, I repeated my question.

"I *do* mind," he said. "Cape Town is too far."

"It isn't by air. The flight only lasts a couple of hours."

169

"What's wrong with Durban? It'll be hotter; and a lot cheaper, being so much nearer. Can you change the bookings?"

"No, I can't," I told him, "It's not that simple. I've already told my mother we'll be staying with your relatives in Cape Town. In case she asks you, I must—"

"My *what*? Did you—"

"Hold on. Let me finish. I—"

He interrupted me again. But whatever he said was inaudible; the line had started crackling. Irritably, I thumped the receiver with the heel of my hand.

"I can't hear you. Speak up," I complained.

He cleared his throat. ". . . I said: are you trying to tell me something?"

"I *am*! If you'll just listen for a moment!"

He was quiet while I explained how the Cohens fitted into my plan. At the end he remained silent, so that I had to ask him if he was still there.

He grunted.

"Well? . . . Say—"

"Your parents might attempt to contact you—what then?"

"Lynn's cousins have been briefed. Lynn rang them this afternoon. They've agreed to cover up for me. And they know where we'll be staying, in case of any emergency."

"You've obviously got it all worked out," he said sourly.

"Except for you. I expected you to be a little more enthusiastic about the idea of spending two weeks alone with me on holiday."

"In *Durban*—I can afford a holiday in Durban. But if you're so dead set on going to Cape Town, there's nothing to stop you going on your own."

170

"Too bloody true," I retorted. "You don't have to put yourself out on my behalf. I can easily find someone else to keep me company." And I slammed the receiver down.

He called me back about two hours later. I was in the bath. Mark came and hammered on the door, which I had taken the precaution to lock because I didn't want anyone bursting in and discovering me in tears.

"It's Dave on the phone," Mark shouted through the keyhole.

My throat was blocked with phlegm. "W-who?"

"Hurry up, man." He rattled the doorknob. "Dave's on the phone."

"Tell him I'm out," I said.

"W-h-a-t?"

"All right!" I yelled. *"I'm coming!"*

I splashed cold water over my face, wrapped myself in a towel, and squelched along the passage. Mark had left the receiver dangling a few inches above the floor at the end of its cord. It was swinging slowly back and forth, like a portentous pendulum. As I caught it up, the mouthpiece banged against the edge of the table. But I didn't apologize for the noise it must have made in Dave's ear.

"I was in the bath. What did you want?" I said grumpily.

"I want *you.* So I'll come to Cape Town. Okay?" A slight slurring of his syllables aroused my suspicions.

"Dave—are you sloshed?"

"Sloshed? You kidding? I'm sober as a cold stone . . . well, almost."

"What have you been drinking?"

"The 'Ruby Vintage' of Omar Khayyám. *The Rubái-yát*—know it? 'Ah, my Belovèd, fill the Cup that clears

171

Today of past Regrets and future Fears. . . .' I reckon
he had the right philosophy. Listen, are we going to Cape
Town, then?"

"Providing you're sure you want—"

"You have my word. I'll even give it to you in writing,
if you like."

"Mmm! I might," I said. His conciliatory cheerfulness
was contagious. "Only I don't know how you do it in
writing."

"You slip it in between the lines."

"Goof!"

"What about preventing pregnant pauses?"

"It's been dealt with. I meant to tell you, Lynn rec-
ommended someone, and I've got an appointment for this
Friday."

"Someone? A doctor?"

"Yes, but I can't say more now."

"I understand," he said. "You aren't in the study."

"That's right."

"Big Ears is listening in?"

"No doubt."

"We'll soon discover. Agree to marry me."

"I beg your pardon?"

"It's for his benefit. Let him hear. Say you'll marry me."

"Oh, I see." I raised my voice. "Marry you? Yes! Yes,
I'd love to. I would, yes. When?"

"Saturday week?"

"Saturday week? Golly! . . . All right, yes. Fine. Why
not? We'll have to elope, though. My mother would never
allow it, so it'll have to be kept very secret."

"We'll take Spoodie with us."

"Spoodie? Of course. We'll take Spoodie with us. I know you gave her to Mark, but he won't miss her. He doesn't really love her."

"I DO!" a voice bellowed. "SHE'S MINE. YOU CAN'T HAVE HER."

"Did you hear that?" I asked Dave.

He laughed. "Tell him I was only joking. I must go now. I need to finish some revision before I'm too squiffy."

"You won't drink any more tonight, will you?" I said sternly.

"I'll ring you tomorrow. Sleep well."

"Wait! Dave"—I cupped my hands round the mouthpiece to prevent my words carrying—"are you certain about Cape Town?"

"I'm certain I love you," he said, and hung up.

My father told me he thought the holiday was a good idea. I could do with a break at the sea before starting university, he said, and added that he trusted Dave to look after me and see that I came to no harm. I was relieved that he didn't ask any awkward questions, as I couldn't have lied to him with equanimity. He pressed some spending money on me—one hundred rands—and made me promise to let him know if I ran short and needed more. It was fortunate that I had caught him in an exceptionally busy period at work, when his mind was preoccupied and he had little time or thought to devote to family matters.

Mark told me bluntly he hoped I would marry in Cape Town because then he could move into my bedroom, which, according to him, was much bigger and nicer than his.

Sophie told me I shouldn't fly down to the Cape. She wanted me to travel by train. With a provocative twinkle in her eye, she said that if God had intended us to fly, he would have given us wings and claws, not flat feet. And he wouldn't have created us on the sixth day. He would have created us on the fifth day, with the birds. Besides which, airplanes were causing the current drought, she claimed. There were too many of them now in the sky, cutting too many holes in the clouds and drying up the air with the heat of their engines.

"But I will pray for you, Miss Rhonda," she said finally, and her humorously sly sidelong glance left me with the uncomfortable feeling that she knew exactly what I would be getting up to on this holiday.

As for my mother, she assiduously avoided mentioning the subject until the last minute. While I was packing my suitcase, she came into my bedroom to ask if I had everything I needed for the trip.

"What about reading matter?" she said.

"I've put in a couple of paperbacks," I told her.

"And for the flight? You might like something light to browse through on the plane. Here, you'd better take these." She dropped two magazines on the bed and went out smartly.

Her hasty exit made me suspicious. I picked up the top magazine and flipped through it. One of the pages was earmarked. It featured a lengthy argument against abortion on religious grounds. The second magazine had an earmarked medical article claiming a possible connection between early sexual experience and cancer of the cervix.

On the reverse side of the page was a detailed account of all the possible health risks associated with the pill.

I checked that I had my month's supply of the pill safely stowed away at the bottom of my shoulder bag and finished my packing. After that I sat down and read the three articles. Then I laid the magazines on the windowsill, where my mother would be sure to find them after my departure in the morning.

eighteen

The Cape of Good Hope. That was the name given to the
Cape peninsula after Bartholomeu Dias had successfully
sailed round it in 1488. At its southernmost tip, two oceans
come together. The warm waters of the Indian Ocean
meet and mingle with the colder waters of the Atlantic.
On my first visit to Cape Town at the age of eight, my
family drove the twenty-odd miles along the spectacular
mountainside coastal drive to witness this oceanic union.
I remember my bitter disappointment in discovering that
the wide expanse of sea, stretching to the horizon from
the cliff face at Cape Point, was a uniform shade of blue.
I had been expecting the separate identities of the two
oceans to be distinguishable by a visible difference in color,
and I felt cheated.

Nevertheless, I did fall in love with Cape Town. My father took me up Table Mountain in the cable car. I stood on the edge of the flat-topped summit, looking down over a sheer drop of several thousand feet at the diminutive toy city nestled between the foot of the mountain and the broad blue curve of Table Bay. It was a hot, sunny day, without a cloud or a breath of wind. The rocky coves and sandy beaches of Cape Town's shore suburbs were fringed with transparent turquoise, deepening to ultramarine beyond the coastline. A man standing next to my father said he had been all over the world, but this was the most beautiful view he had ever seen. I believed him. Influenced by the fairy-tale romance I was currently reading, I decided there and then that when I grew up and met my Prince Charming, we would have our honeymoon in Cape Town.

And now, ten years later, with a red face, I found myself confessing my childish vow to my funny Prince Charming, as we relaxed on the balcony of our hotel bedroom, breathing in the tangy sea air.

"My wish has come true," I said.

"No, it hasn't. We're not married, and I'm not your Prince."

I jostled him. "What are you, then?"

"I'm *me*," he said tersely.

He angled his head round to follow the flight of a sea gull gliding above the railings along the promenade. The slanting blaze of afternoon sunlight lit up the chiseled contour of his cheekbone and jaw; a muscle moved spasmodically at the side of his mouth. He was tense. He had been tense and uncommunicative from the moment we had stepped out of the plane at D. F. Malan Airport.

Perturbed, I asked him if he was all right.

He brushed off the question with a shrug and leaned on the parapet, staring out to sea. "What would you like to do now? Unpack? Or get something to drink?"

"You haven't kissed me yet. That's what I would like. A kiss from you before anything else."

"Not in front of all those people down there."

"Who cares about them?"

"I do."

"Then let's go inside." I tucked my arm through his, snuggling up to him. "Come on, huh? . . . Davie?"

His whole body went taut. "*Don't* call me that."

"What? Davie?"

"It isn't my name."

"Sorry, I'm sure!" I said, and flounced into the room.

Our suitcases were propped up against each other at the bottom end of the bed. I moved them out of the way and flung myself down on the candlewick bedspread. It had an alien, faintly musty smell. I cast my eye round the room. Earlier it had looked cozily inviting and intimate to me; now it felt impersonal, its atmosphere intimidating. I was besieged by sudden doubts about spending two weeks confined here with Dave in his present mood. Cupping my hands over my eyes, I willed myself to relax.

He must have crossed the room very quietly, because I didn't hear him. I only felt the mattress give under his weight. He pulled my hands away and covered my face with kisses. I opened my mouth to protest, but his lips sealed mine. I struggled for a second, then acquiesced, responding to the fervor of his passion. We wrestled out of our clothes. He made love to me wordlessly, with a tense desperation that I felt in the trembling rigidity of his forceful, sinewy body as he moved over me.

His climax was shattering. I was afraid his convulsions would tear him apart, and held him in a fierce protective stranglehold. It was some time before I realized that the sobbing noises he was making were sounds of grief. His face was pushed into the pillow. I touched his cheek and found it wet.

But he couldn't tell me why he was crying. He started choking when he tried to speak. I cradled his head on my breast, aching with a new, raw depth of tenderness in my feeling for him. He finally quieted and lay still. Our bodies were bonded together with sweat; as he maneuvered himself up on his forearms, our skin parted stickily with a small tearing sound that I felt deep inside myself. His eyes smiled into mine.

"Feeling better now?" I asked.

He sighed. "I wish we could stay like this forever."

"We will," I stated categorically. ". . . Hey, what's so funny? Why are you laughing at me?"

"Because you're lovely. . . . And because I love you. . . . And just because." His speech was thickened by the huskiness in his voice. Caressing my cheek, he said, "Would you like a cigarette break?"

"I'd like a glass of champagne."

"We haven't any."

"We have. I brought a bottle with me. It's hidden under my coat in the carrier bag. Do you want to fetch it?"

"Not now." He kissed me. "We'll celebrate after."

"After what?"

"After we've completed our unfinished business to the satisfaction of both parties."

"I thought we had," I said.

He saved his breath and began to prove to me otherwise, starting at my feet. It took a deliciously long time, this unfinished business, and his patient determination paid off. I certainly had cause to celebrate afterwards.

"What happened to you?" he asked, laughing, as I lay limply in his arms, moaning indulgently now that the tidal wave had receded.

He didn't expect an answer, and he didn't receive one. All he got from me was a smile of blissful repletion.

We savored our champagne in bed, watching the sky outside the window turn from apricot to salmon pink to dusky lavender. It was a moment of profound happiness because I knew then, without a shadow of doubt in my mind, that I wanted to share the rest of my life with him. I wanted to marry him, and have his child too, one day. One day . . . not yet. I wasn't in any hurry; we had all the time in the world ahead of us.

nineteen

The two weeks passed far too quickly. Yet we did very little with our time—very little in public, that is. We swam every day at least once, but we never basked on the sand after our dip. All the beaches within walking distance were crowded, and although that didn't bother me, it affected Dave. He seemed unable to relax when there were people around us, preferring to go back to the hotel and sunbathe on our balcony. We practically lived on the balcony. I didn't mind. It was a suntrap and had certain practical and persuasive advantages over the beach—not least being the proximity of our double bed.

After dinner in the evenings, we usually went for a stroll on the seafront. One humid, starry night we walked along the coast road as far as Camps Bay. We paddled in the sea and kidded about on the dark beach, which we had all to ourselves. In the middle of a mock wrestling match, Dave tripped over backwards. I quickly jumped on him and pinned him down.

"Got you now," I crowed. "And I'm going to have my way with you, my lad."

"Fantastic." He wriggled his hips suggestively. "Well, what are you waiting for? I'm ready."

"Will you take me up Table Mountain tomorrow?"

"No."

I settled my full weight on his stomach. "Say yes."

"You're squashing me," he groaned.

"Say yes."

"No," he said.

"But I want to look at the view."

"What for? You've already seen it."

"Not with you. It's such a romantic view, I want to—"

"Romantic?" He brought his head up angrily. "Christ! You don't know bloody Cape Town, do you?"

"And I suppose you do?" I retaliated. "You've been here once, you told me; but you're so clever, you know all there is to know about it." Incensed, I levered myself off him and started back across the sand in a huff.

He eventually followed and caught up with me about half a mile along the road. The return journey to the hotel seemed endless because we weren't speaking. In our room, I undressed and climbed into bed. Dave went and stood on the balcony for a long time. I pretended to be asleep when he finally joined me. His hand groped for my shoulder under the sheet.

"Are you awake?" he whispered. "There's something you don't . . . I want to talk . . . Rhonda?"

I lay very still, waiting for him to say more. I guess I was waiting for him to say he was sorry. But then he swore softly and rolled over away from me. It was ages before his breathing settled into a slow, regular rhythm.

Self-contempt and remorse kept me awake. I listened to the sounds from the outside world: the incessant droning of the surf, punctuated intermittently by the discordant shriek of late-night traffic accelerating past the hotel. A door slammed somewhere along the corridor. Dave whimpered in his sleep and began grinding his teeth. A tap was dripping in the bathroom. I got up to switch it off.

When I returned, Dave was lying in the middle of the bed with his face half on my pillow. As I lifted the sheet, his body twitched a little and his hands reached out. I snuggled in between his arms.

He sighed drowsily. ". . . Love . . . me."

My throat was smarting. I kissed him, and he smiled without opening his eyes. He wasn't fully conscious.

"Don't leave me," he mumbled.

"Never!" I vowed.

I went to sleep, hugging him, our faces close together on the pillow, nose to nose; like Mark and Spoodie that traumatic night after the party in Turffontein.

He woke me in the morning with a cup of coffee. He had already washed and shaved, and was dressed in a pair of fresh white jeans, a cream shirt, and a smart sports jacket.

"It's a terrific day," he said, ripping the curtains wide

183

open and filling the room with an eye-searing dazzle of sunlight. "So wakey, wakey, rise and riz, if you aren't sitting up in two seconds flat, you won't get a kiss."

I squinted at him groggily. "You're in a good mood. But what are you wearing those snazzy clothes for?"

"I can't go up Table Mountain in my swimming trunks, can I—or hire a car?"

"Hire a car?"

"Ya. We'll hire a car for the day and drive to the cable station. It'll save us going into Cape Town."

"What's wrong with going into Cape Town?"

"Who wants to?" He shrugged.

"I do," I said, and his face fell. "I need to buy a few presents."

He took his cup and went to refill it from the pot on the hotel tray. Guiltily I contemplated his back. Here he was being terribly sweet and putting himself out for me, and I wasn't being in the least bit appreciative.

The color of his cord jacket was a rich shade of caramel. He looked very elegant and handsome in it. Because he had such straight shoulders, his clothes always hung well on him. Leaping off the bed, I ran up and hugged him from behind.

"You're adorable, Dave. And you're mine. And you know how I would like to spend today?" I rubbed myself against him. "Wouldn't you?"

"You're making me spill my coffee."

"Never mind your coffee. Put it down. Come back to bed."

He braced himself, resisting my efforts to turn him. "What about Table Mountain? You said you—"

184

"I've changed my mind. We've only a few days left. Time is too precious to waste on sight-seeing excursions."

"Now you tell me," he grumbled, "after I've got myself all togged—"

"I'll help you undress."

Caressingly, I slid my hands under his jacket and began to unfasten his shirt buttons. He jumped away.

"You're mad!" he shouted at me.

As if that wasn't shock enough, he made a sudden rush for the door. My heart contracted.

"W-where are you g— Dave!"

He fumbled at the lock and wrenched the door open before he looked round. The rotter! He had a wolfish grin on his face.

"I'm hanging out the 'Do Not Disturb' notice," he said.

twenty

I left the shopping I had to do until the day of our departure. Our flight was in the afternoon. The hotel manager kindly said that we needn't vacate our room before then, as it wasn't going to be in use that night.

I told Dave he didn't have to come with me into Cape Town. "You could spend the morning sunbathing on the balcony," I suggested. "I'll be back as quick as I can."

He was sprawled in one of the two easy chairs in the room, his leg hooked over the armrest, his nose buried in a science fiction paperback. I prodded his foot with mine.

"Dave, I'm talking to you!"

"I heard you," he muttered.

"Can't you put that book down for a minute? You've

had two weeks to read it. Are you coming with me, or not?"

He turned over the page. "Why don't you just send Lynn's cousin something when you get back to Johannesburg?"

"Because I want to buy Lynn a present as well—I told you! And I might also look for a Christmas present for Mark while I'm at it."

"You'll be hours, then," he groused.

"I won't. I've a rough idea of what I'm after. It shouldn't take me long if I can find the right shops."

A small winged insect settled on his shin. As he kicked his leg, the muscles in his thigh flexed; I stroked my fingers over their bronzed firmness appreciatively. He frowned at my hand, then up at me.

"It would be a lot more fun if you came too," I said. "But you don't feel like it, do you?"

He returned to his reading. "No, I want to finish this."

He had been moody and taciturn since breakfast. I was a bit on edge myself, resenting the thought of having to pack up and go home and part from him. I was most dreading the actual moment of our parting. I kept trying not to think ahead.

I changed into a skirt and put on some makeup. He didn't even glance up when I called good-bye from across the room.

"Be good," I said, and, receiving no answer, banged the door after me.

At the bus stop, I suddenly saw him striding towards me. He broke into a run as a bus appeared. "Get on; it's the right one," he shouted.

Once we had found two empty seats and paid the fare, I asked him what had made him decide to come, after all.

"Does there have to be a reason?" he said unhelpfully, staring round me out the window.

I gave up the attempt to communicate with him, and we sat in silence the rest of the way into the city center. From the terminal, we wandered up Adderley Street. While I gazed in all the shopwindows, Dave slouched, grim faced, at my elbow, contemplating the passersby. I left him smoking a cigarette and popped into a department store. Lynn's present was easy. I bought her a bottle of expensive French perfume I knew she would like. Choosing a gift for the Cohens proved more difficult; I emerged finally without one.

Dave had moved and was standing on the corner, watching three small barefoot Colored boys chasing each other round a lamppost. I watched them too for a couple of moments, fascinated by the racial mixture that showed in their faces. The smallest boy, whose impish expression reminded me of Mark, had a pale freckled complexion with frizzy African hair. The middle-sized boy had Indian features. The biggest boy, who was also the darkest, had slanted Oriental eyes and curly brown locks. He barged into a young White woman carrying a load of parcels. She shook her finger at him. He ran off, laughing, with his two companions.

Dave hadn't seen me as yet. He jumped when I touched his sleeve.

"Did I startle you?" I said. "Sorry about that."

His eyes veered away from mine and scanned the faces of the people about us. The pre-Christmas rush had started.

Necklaces of lights and colored illuminations festooned Adderley Street; the sidewalks were congested with shoppers. I would have enjoyed the holiday crowds and the general atmosphere of festive excitement if Dave hadn't been so immured in himself. Taking his arm to cross the road, I felt as though I were holding on to a suit of armor.

It was developing into another sweltering day. My throat was rough and dry. I suggested finding somewhere quiet to sit down and have a drink. Our search led us past the canopied flower market. After the fiendish heat and the fumes of the traffic, the cool vapor of sweet, moist scents was like a breath of heaven. I asked Dave to stop and went nearer, sniffing appreciatively.

One of the Colored women, sitting in a row in the shade, bobbed up and tried to sell me a bunch of the huge-headed yellow dahlias I was admiring. She was very persistent. Unable to understand her Cape dialect, I turned to Dave for help. Misinterpreting my gesture, the woman thrust the dahlias towards him. He stared closely at her, then past her at the other flower sellers in the background, carefully scrutinizing each of their faces. The woman was talking to him now.

"Do you understand her?" I asked.

"We don't want any flowers," he growled. "So come on." He pulled me away roughly.

The control I had been exerting over myself snapped then; I squared up to him. "I've had enough of this," I said acrimoniously. "I can't take any more of you and your mood. It's our last day together, and you've spoiled it all by behaving like a—like a—" I never had time to finish. His arms lunged out and lassoed me, and I was literally swept off my feet in a violent embrace. I gulped out, "What are you *doing*?"

He set me down. "I care about you!" he exclaimed savagely, gripping my shoulders. "I care about you!" His body sagged as he let his breath go and relaxed suddenly. The wildness went out of his eyes. In a quieter, hoarse voice, he said, "Whatever happens, I *love* you. You must believe me."

My resentment melted into a warm glow of forgiveness. People were observing us, but I didn't give a damn. I thrust my face up and he kissed me. The kiss was inflammatory; I squeezed him passionately. He groaned.

"Let's go home. I hate this place. I want to be alone with you. I need to be close to you. Let's go back to our room." His eyes caressed me. "Do you want to?"

I smiled at him. "Can't you tell?"

"What about the rest of your shopping?"

"It's not important. It can wait. But I must have a quick milk shake first. I'm parched, and my throat feels like sandpaper."

I can remember, in haunting detail, what we talked about in the snack bar. Holding hands across the table, eyes devouring each other, we discussed the future. Our future. We decided that somehow or other we had to find a way of being able to actually live together as soon as possible. Then, after three years, when we had both graduated, we would leave South Africa and settle in London. These major decisions were made in the time it took us to down our milk shakes.

We rose to leave. Hugging Dave's arm, I blurted out

with emotional impulsiveness, "And someday, you know, I'd like to have your child."

It wasn't that he said anything. It was how he looked at me, as if I had suddenly slammed an open door in his face.

Uncomprehending, I asked, "Why are you—I didn't mean *now*, Dave. I certainly don't want a child yet, if that's what's—"

"I've got to pay the bill," he cut in, yanking his arm from my grasp.

I followed him to the counter.

"I thought you liked kids. Don't you?" I asked him as he pocketed the change.

"I do. Are we going home now?"

"Yes, please," I said.

He took the hand I gave him, and we left the snack bar. But the feeling between us had altered; he was tense again, and I couldn't understand why. Puzzling it over in my mind, I probably wouldn't have noticed the two figures huddled on the sidewalk outside if one of them hadn't jumped up and accosted Dave.

"Kissmas, baas. Kissmas, please, baas."

The speaker was a young Colored girl in her early teens. That was all I registered about her, because it was the crippled woman, propped up against the wall behind her, who caught my attention. The woman's legs were deformed and badly scarred. The sight of them turned my stomach. I focused instead on her face. It was a little, wizened face, and it interested me because its physiognomy and wrinkled yellowish-brown complexion clearly revealed Hottentot blood in its ancestry.

191

The woman rattled her begging tin, grinning optimistically. She had an enchanting grin that animated all the crinkles in her cheeks and enlivened her eyes.

"Kissmas, baas. Happy *Kissmas,"* she said to Dave.

"Give her some money," I told him. "You've got change, haven't you?"

It was then that I saw he was staring in mute horror at the woman's mutilated limbs. I nudged him, but he didn't seem to be aware of me. His gaze was now riveted on the face grinning up at him. I felt a touch on my wrist.

"Please, madam," the girl appealed to me. "Please give me money for my mother. For happy *Kissmas."*

I opened my bag hurriedly and scratched around in it to find my purse. Embarrassed, I muttered, "I don't think I have any coins," and I glanced at Dave, knowing he had the change from the bill in his pocket.

With the same fixed expression of shock, he was staring into the girl's face. I looked at her and for the first time noticed her eyes. I wasn't able to make any sense of what I saw; my panic was instinctive. Plucking a one-rand note from my purse, I threw it at the startled girl, seized hold of Dave, and dragged him after me across the street.

He came willingly enough, offering no resistance. But when I spoke to him, he gazed right through me, as if I weren't there. He appeared to be oblivious of my presence, and slightly disoriented—like a person suffering from delayed concussion. He kept bumping into people and objects, even though I was supporting him by the arm.

I wasn't in a very rational state myself. My one clear thought was that I must get us to the hotel as fast as possible. I headed for Adderley Street in the hope of hailing a taxi. Near the flower market, Dave suddenly stopped in his tracks.

"Chr-ist . . . !" A shudder ran through him. "I've *got* to go back!"

"We are," I said. "I'm taking you back, Dave, it's okay. This is the way."

He twisted round, knocking me off balance. Viciously, he barked, "Stay here!" and plunged into the crowd.

I set off in pursuit. But he had a head start and was already lost to view. An ominous, unintelligible fear slackened my pace as I retraced the route to the snack bar. It was in a narrow side street that carried hardly any traffic, and there weren't many people about. I spotted Dave on the opposite sidewalk as soon as I turned the corner.

He was with the Colored girl and her mother, and someone else who hadn't been there earlier—a swarthy-skinned Colored boy of about sixteen. I was out of hearing range, but the boy appeared to be threatening Dave. Then Dave turned and bent over the crippled form on the ground. I halted on the curb, held back from going any closer by my stupefaction at seeing Dave grasp the woman's outstretched hand and press it to his cheek.

Practically in the same moment, the Colored boy sprang at Dave, grabbed him by the collar, and hauled him upright. It all happened too fast to comprehend. And the whole thing was over in a few seconds. Dave seemed to be trying to reason with his aggressor. But the boy shoved him aside, stooped, lifted the woman easily into his arms, and bore her away, pushing the girl in front of him. Above his shoulder, the woman's face looked back at Dave; I could see she was crying.

Dave had collapsed against the wall and was holding his head in his hands. As I started over the road, he straightened up and stared after the disappearing figures. Then he staggered forward and broke into a wild run in the opposite direction. Shouting his name, I gave chase. He vanished round the far corner; by the time I reached it, he was nowhere in sight.

I tramped the streets searching for him. Eventually I persuaded myself that he must have returned to the hotel. I rushed to the bus stop, running most of the way.

Our room was empty. A sweeping glance revealed that it was exactly as I had left it. I checked the balcony and the bathroom. Feeling faint, I gulped some water at the basin, which eased my sore throat but made me queasy. Tottering to the bed, I fell in a heap on it.

Where was he? In less than two hours' time, we had to depart for the airport. What if he hadn't come by then? What would I do? Ring the police? Ring Lynn's cousin? But what would I say to her? And what could she do, anyway? . . . *Oh God! . . . Please! . . . Where WAS he?*

I felt myself to be on the verge of hysteria and sat up shakily. Hugging my knees, I cast my mind back over the incident, hunting for clues as to its meaning. There had to be a connection between Dave's reluctance to come to Cape Town and the Colored beggar woman. The connection had to be something traumatic. So much was evident. I did know of a traumatic event in Dave's past life that remained shrouded in mystery because he had never been able to talk to me about it: the death of his brother and two sisters. Perhaps their death and the Colored woman's injuries were linked. Perhaps . . . perhaps Dave and his family and the woman had all been involved in a tragic accident in Cape Town . . . a fatal road accident? That would explain Dave's shock at seeing the woman and his irrational behavior. It would explain the Colored boy's animosity towards him. It would explain . . . well, everything. But where was he? *Oh God! Why didn't he come?*

I went out on the balcony and scanned the street and the promenade. My panic erupted in a burst of anger. How could he do this to me? Regardless of his state of mind, he must realize that I would be worried sick about him. And he must be aware of the time; he had a watch. What could he be thinking of—not me, obviously! Well, I couldn't wait for him any longer. I had to pack up and get myself ready. If he missed the flight, it was his own fault!

I raced round the room, gathering up our scattered belongings in a sudden frenzy. When I had packed my suitcase, I started to fill Dave's more slowly and carefully, folding his clothes neatly. Every once in a while, I dashed out to the balcony to see if there was any sign of him. Having closed and locked both suitcases, I left them on the bed and tidied up the room. Then I sat down and stared at the telephone. After consulting my watch for the umpteenth time, I dialed the Cohens' number. But as soon as a voice answered, I rang off. I was still clutching the receiver when I heard the sound of footsteps.

He came in, closed the door, and leaned on it, looking at me.

Whatever I had been going to say lodged in my throat. His clothes were disheveled. His face was streaked with

195

dirt. The bottoms of his trousers were wringing wet, and a layer of damp sand clung to his shoes. Out of the side pocket of his jacket protruded a brandy bottle. And he didn't utter a word. He just stood there, regarding me impassively.

His manner, his appearance, his silence, sent a little cold shiver of apprehension down my spine. I replaced the receiver.

"Where the hell have you been?"

"Sitting on a 'Whites Only' beach."

"You're drunk!"

"Ya, I am."

No apology. Not even a hint of contrition in his voice for having needlessly driven me half out of my mind with worry. The tension inside me exploded.

"*Do you realize* . . . I don't suppose you care that I've been going frant —*Sitting on a beach? . . . Christ!* And here I was, thinking something awful must have—thinking you might have had an accident or been knifed by that Colored thug who—"

"Thug?"

"I saw him threaten you. I saw the whole thing, so it's no use pretending—just bloody explain to me, Dave, what the beggar woman, the cripple, has to do with you, because—"

"She's my mother." There was a movement in his face, a contraction round the mouth, that looked as if he was trying to control a laugh.

"This *isn't* funny!" I yelled at him.

He shut his eyes and let his head flop back, leaning his

full weight on the door. The muscles in his throat strained as he attempted to speak. But only a hoarse, muffled sound came out. Clenching his fingers, he swallowed.

"She was knocked down by a hit-and-run driver three years ago." He slammed his fists into the wood behind him. "Three years ago, and I never knew. I never knew. . . ." He punched the door even harder.

I gazed in alarm at the flecks of blood on his knuckles. Almost timidly, I asked, "Dave, who is she?"

"I told you." His eyes opened. There were tears in them. "My mother," he said in a voice like a sheet of ice splintering.

The thought flashed through my mind that he had lost his reason and that I shouldn't provoke him. I spoke to him gently.

"She isn't your mother, Dave. Your mother is in Johann—"

"*Shut up!* . . . Shut up and listen will you. I'm not that drunk. I'm trying . . . dammit, I'm trying to tell you who I am. I was born here, in Cape Town. Those people are my real family. That guy you call a thug is my brother. My brother and sisters aren't dead. I was lying when I said they were. He's my brother, and that girl you saw is one of my sisters."

My blood ran cold as I remembered my jolt on noticing the girl's unusual eyes: incandescent gold-green eyes—like Dave's. "But she's Colored," I burst out incredulously.

"So am I," he said.

"You can't be," I gasped at him. "You can't be! You're lying now—you must be! You're White."

"A pass-White." He gave me a horrible grimace. "I look White. Aren't I lucky."

I felt as if I had been struck by a bolt of lightning. I was paralyzed. He pulled himself up from the door and stood, balancing unsteadily on his feet.

Tonelessly, he said, "So now you know about me."

He waited. With horror, I stared across the room, seeing not his face but the faces of his family. The coffee-complexioned, green-eyed face of the girl. The Hottentot, crosshatched face of the woman. The dusky, African face of the boy. They were all *dark* faces. *His* family. *Colored!* The full implications rained on me suddenly like hammer blows.

I had been to bed with—my naked body had been touched and fondled by a non-White! . . . I might be carrying his—if by some freak chance I was pregnant, my baby would be Colored!

An attack of nausea swamped me. As I stuffed my hand over my mouth, the figure at the door made a movement.

"And now *I* know about *you*," he said, and he swore at me. Then he seemed to gather himself up before he plunged forward.

A stool was in his path. He kicked it, sending it crashing into the back of a chair. I cowered, petrified, while he reeled on towards me. He stumbled against the edge of the mattress, and I brought my arms up to defend myself. His lunge went past me; he was reaching for his suitcase in the middle of the bed. He lifted it over my head and dropped it on the floor. His face came very close to mine. His eyes blazed with enmity; but in their depths was a look that will haunt me for the rest of my life: a look of irreparable hurt.

"It beats me why I ever fell for you," he said. "You're only skindeep." Then he picked up the suitcase and lurched out with it.

My stomach heaved. I ran into the bathroom and was violently sick.

twenty-one

I remember nothing of the flight home. At Jan Smuts Airport, I rang Lynn's house. Fortunately, she was there. Joel was with her. I didn't have to explain anything over the telephone; Lynn picked up the state I was in, and she and Joel drove straight out to the airport to fetch me. They took me to Joel's flat in Hillbrow.

My sinuses felt as though they were coated with chili powder. My head was throbbing. I was feverish and shaky. I couldn't talk at all in the car. Lynn didn't try to force me to. She tucked me up on the sofa in Joel's living room and fussed over me. Joel brought me a hot drink of lemon and honey and whisky. I gagged on the first mouthful, but I managed to swallow the rest down and felt a little better for it.

I started to talk then. Once I started, I couldn't stop. My account of the scene between Dave and me must have been very garbled and incoherent; I was slightly delirious, I think. At some point, Lynn interrupted me.

"Poor Dave," she said.

Joel rounded on her. "Now do you see what I mean? This bloody country!"

Lynn spoke to him sharply, and they began arguing. Their voices were unintelligible to me. I felt like someone waking up from an anesthetic after an operation; my mind was confused, but I was becoming conscious of an intensifying, deep pain—a raw, throbbing sense of loss.

"He should have . . . why couldn't he have told me before?"

The effort of speaking brought tears to my eyes. I clasped my throat, struggling to swallow. Lynn and Joel had fallen silent and were staring at me. Joel lunged up from his chair.

"It's blatantly obvious to me why he couldn't," he said contemptuously, and left the room.

Lynn pulled an apologetic face. "Don't mind him, Rhond. Is your throat very sore? I'll fix you another drink."

Taking my glass, she went out to join Joel in the kitchen, shutting the door after her. I had a vision of Dave staggering out with his suitcase, the door clicking closed behind him. And six hours too late, I realized, with a suffocating feeling of desolation, that he meant more to me than anything else in my life. I didn't think any further than that. I unpacked Lynn's present and placed it next to the telephone. As I was putting on my coat in the hall, Lynn appeared.

201

"That parcel is for you. I'm going back to Cape Town," I informed her.

"Over my dead body." She stuck her hands on her hips. "You aren't going anywhere, Rhond. You're ill."

"I'm *going*! . . . Don't worry about me. It's just a cold."

"Just a cold!" She felt my forehead. "You're running a bladdy temperature."

I tried to reach the front door. She pulled me back, calling for Joel. He double-locked the door and slid the safety chain across.

"You're out of your mind," he told me.

"Please!" I appealed to him. "Can't you see? I have to find Dave. I *have* to. I'm not even sure if he's got enough money."

"It's a bit bloody late to think of that now," he said.

"I know . . ." My knees were buckling. "I know it's too late, but I must find him and—"

"You should be in bed," he said more kindly. "We'll take you home."

"Do you want to go home?" Lynn asked me.

I shook my head. I started to speak, then my legs collapsed under me.

I only vaguely remember Joel carrying me through the flat to the spare room, and Lynn undressing me and helping me into bed. A little later, Lynn brought me a bowl of soup and told me she had rung my mother.

"I said you had missed your plane and would be flying back tomorrow instead. I hope I did right?"

"Thanks," I rasped. "Was she difficult?"

"Your ma? No. She sounded in a flap because your pa and Mark are setting off at dawn to drive to Durban, and

202

they haven't begun packing yet. They'll be gone for a few days, so at least you won't have them to contend with. . . . Come on, Rhond, eat your soup."

"I'm sorry." Tears were spilling down my cheeks. "But I've *got* to find Dave."

"You will. When you're better. Now eat your soup. Joel has slipped out to the emergency chemist to—"

"Joel? . . . Oh God! Lynn, I've spoiled your whole evening together. I'm so sorry."

"Rubbish. You've done me a favor really. Joel wasn't planning to spend the evening with me." Her smile was a sad clown's smile.

I pushed the bowl away. "Not *you* as well," I croaked. "I thought you and Joel were happy."

"We *were*. I guess we still are. Only I'm taking up too much of his time, or so he says. It would be different, perhaps, if I shared his political commitment and was able to help him more in all his anti-Apartheid activities. I do try to help, but I'm not certain I want to become very involved. It's too bladdy dangerous. He's under surveillance, you know, by the security police. They keep a watch on this flat and the phone is tapped. Joel doesn't let it get to him, but it scares the hell out of me. I'm scared for him also. I mean I love the guy. I'm not crazy to see him end up in solitary confinement. Shit! Maybe I'm just a coward. I don't know. . . . Hey, can't you finish this soup? Aren't you hungry, Rhond?"

I was lying down with the pillow pulled over my eyes. I felt physically incapable of answering her. She tucked the blankets in, switched off the light, and left me to myself.

I drifted in and out of a restless, dream-plagued sleep. It was quite late when Joel and Lynn went to bed. I woke to the mumble of their voices coming through the wall from the next room. They were speaking softly so as not to disturb me, but they were obviously quarreling. I believed they were arguing about me.

Stealing out of bed, I padded to the window. There was a drop of at least sixty feet to the narrow concrete alleyway below. I unfastened the latch and pushed the window. It opened wide enough to squeeze through. Leaning on the sill, I thought about Dave, and about my life, and about a lot of things. I came to no conclusions other than that I was probably catching pneumonia, standing there in a cold draft. Shivering, emotionally numb with exhaustion, I closed the window and crawled back into bed.

twenty-two

Lynn insisted on coming with me. Joel said we could borrow his car. I looked up the address in the telephone directory, and we set out straight after breakfast. My cold had settled in my chest, but my head felt slightly clearer.

We took a few wrong turns before we found the house in Turffontein. It was a small, old squat brick building, with a faded red corrugated-iron roof. Three shrub roses and a hydrangea competed for space in the pocket-handkerchief garden. A jungle of potted plants on the low, dark front veranda screened the windows of the house. The closed front door had a forbidding air. I sat in the car and contemplated it, trying to pluck up my courage.

"Perhaps they aren't at home," I said half hopefully.

"Are you scared, Rhond? It isn't too late to change your mind. You don't have to go in."

"I do." I unfastened my seat belt. "But you can stay here, if you like."

She pulled on the hand brake. "No fear. I'll be right behind you."

The woman who opened the door was short and stout and gray, and wore spectacles. Her manner didn't strike me as friendly.

"Mrs. Schwartz?" My voice squeaked like a mouse.

"Ya." She cast a suspicious eye at the two of us. "Ya, I'm Mrs. Schwartz."

"I'm a friend of Dave's. I'm Rhonda. I don't know if he—"

"Rhonda . . . !" Her hand flew to her breast. She stepped back inside the door. I was afraid she was going to close it on me. But then she said, "I know who you are. You better come inside."

The hallway was cramped. Lynn, squashed up against me, was breathing down my neck. I introduced her to Mrs. Schwartz, who was looking me over with an uncomfortably sharp gaze. I felt like a prisoner in the dock.

"Why have you come here?" Mrs. Schwartz asked me.

If Lynn hadn't been blocking my escape, I might have turned tail and fled. I started stammering.

"Have you come to see Dave?"

A surge of hope freed my tongue. "Is—is he back?"

Something gave way in her face. Her harsh expression crumpled. She wasn't formidable at all; she was a little old lady, struggling to conceal her pain from me.

"He won't be back," she said. "He telephoned from

Cape Town last night. I know what happened down there."

"It's all my fault," I blurted out. "I'm sorry, Mrs. Schwartz." Tears were stinging my eyes. "I don't expect you to forgive me. But *please* will you tell me where he is? I've got to find him."

She shook her head. And then she put her arms round me; I can only imagine what it cost her to do it. I believe I loved her from that moment.

"You look ill, my child."

"I have a cold," I told her. "I hope I won't give it to you."

"I don't catch colds. I'm too old. You must rub Vicks on your chest. Come and sit down in the kitchen. I'll make us some tea."

She apologized for her husband's absence and explained that he was in his furniture workshop a few blocks away, finishing off a child's rocking horse that had to be delivered over the weekend.

"I've always wanted to meet you both," I said. "It hurt me that Dave never invited me here. I couldn't understand why he didn't—I still can't."

A smile of pain pinched her lips as she filled the three cups from the teapot. "You want to understand? You want me to try and help you understand?"

"Please."

Her eyes searched me. I realized I was attempting to hide behind my hair, and swept it back so that she could see whatever there was to see in my face.

"All right, my child. I'll tell you." She sat down on the chair Lynn had pulled out for her. "I'll tell you all about my Dave," she said. And she did.

Dawie was the name his mother, Elsa, gave him when he was born. He was the second of her four children. But he was her favorite because he was fair-skinned. Elsa worked for Mrs. Schwartz and her husband, who were then living in Cape Town; she was employed by Mrs. Schwartz on a part-time basis, doing her housework three days a week. Over a period of months, she came to trust Mrs. Schwartz sufficiently to start confiding in her. She talked about her "troubles" as a widow with a young family, trying to make ends meet financially. She talked about her "troubles" with one of the other White madams she worked for, who treated her badly. She talked about her children. Increasingly, she talked about her "best child," Dawie, and her hopes for his future. What those hopes were was not made clear to Mrs. Schwartz until the afternoon Elsa produced a photograph.

"He looks White, don't he?" she said proudly.

Mrs. Schwartz had agreed that he did; although, as she told us, the little boy's light complexion had escaped her notice because she had been mesmerized by his mischievously enchanting smile.

"He *is* White," Elsa informed her. "It says so on his birth certificate. I'll show you."

She had brought the document with her. The surname on it was different from Elsa's. She said it was her White sister's married name. Noting Mrs. Schwartz's understandable bafflement, she then went on to explain about her family tree.

In the early 1950s, when the Population Registration Act was implemented, Elsa's family had suffered the same fate as many other families at the time. Approximately

208

half of its members had been arbitrarily classified Colored, the other half White, with the inevitable tragic consequences for the family as a whole. Elsa's pale-skinned older sister had been one of the lucky ones. She had qualified for White status and so, fortunately, had the man she was living with, which meant that their relationship could continue legally. They had subsequently got married in a White church. But they were forced to remain childless through fear that their Colored blood would come out in a child. It was this sister and her husband whose names were down on Dawie's birth certificate as his parents, Elsa explained.

"You mustn't tell nobody," she beseeched Mrs. Schwartz. "I trust you. I can open my heart to you. I want the best for him. I want him to grow up White. I am telling you because I want you to help him, please. I want you to learn him to read and write, and talk like White peoples."

Elsa was in a terrible predicament. Being almost illiterate herself, she was determined to make certain her children were educated. Her eldest child was already at school. Dawie was then seven and fretting to be allowed to go to school with his big sister. But as a White child, he couldn't be registered at his sister's Colored school. Not that the inferior educational facilities available in overcrowded Colored schools were part of Elsa's plans for Dawie. She was resolved to register him at a White school. Yet how could she do so without the authorities discovering his home background? That was her dilemma.

The only solution, as she saw it, was to pack Dawie off to live with her White sister for the duration of his school years. But she didn't trust her sister, she said. And so she didn't know what she was going to do. She was asking God to send her luck. In the meantime, would Mrs. Schwartz give Dawie lessons at her house and "learn him to read books and make sums and write nice"?

The lessons continued for several months, by the end of which time the Schwartzes' house had become a second home to Dawie. He was spending every weekday there, and sometimes also staying overnight, with Elsa's blessing. Mrs. Schwartz told her neighbors that he was the son of a friend who was out at work all day. Elsa made sure that he was never seen approaching or leaving the house with her.

"Joseph—my husband—and I were so happy," Mrs. Schwartz confessed to Lynn and me. "Dawie had become like our own boy to us."

"Like your own boy? You already had a son, then?" Lynn asked her.

"I wish! No, we couldn't have children. We hoped to— very much. But I had to have an operation and it made it not possible."

"How awful for you," Lynn sympathized.

Mrs. Schwartz smiled. "God sent us Dawie instead."

If God's hand was in all this, it was a very heavy hand as far as Elsa was concerned. She arrived on Mrs. Schwartz's front doorstep one evening in tears. Instead of sending her the luck she had been asking for, God had sent Elsa yet another "trouble" in the form of a surprise visit from her White sister. Elsa's report of the visit was hysterical and inarticulate, but Mrs. Schwartz gathered the sister was now claiming to have discovered that her husband had fathered Dawie—an allegation Elsa denied. The sister apparently refused to believe her, however, and in a spirit of revengeful jealousy was threatening to claim Dawie as her son and take him away from Elsa.

"She don't want him. She don't love him," Elsa sobbed. "She doing it just to hurt me bad."

"Then it's likely she won't actually take him," Mrs. Schwartz tried to comfort her. "She's only saying she will to upset you."

But Elsa remained inconsolable.

"Well, what do you want me to do?" asked Mrs. Schwartz. "You want me to speak to your sister for you?"

That wasn't what Elsa wanted. She had obviously thought the whole thing through on the long journey by train and two buses from the Colored township, and had reached a painful decision in her own mind. Right from the very beginning, she had always known that if she was to realize her ambition for Dawie, she would have to part with him sooner or later. Now, it seemed the moment had been forced on her prematurely, and she had no other choice but to resign herself to the fact. This was why she was weeping, she admitted to Mrs. Schwartz.

"I know I must give up my baby now. I want the best for him. He must grow up White, so I want to give him to you. Not my sister. I trust you. I know you will look after him nice for me and give him a good life."

It took nearly a year to arrange everything and legalize the adoption, which required the cooperation of Elsa's sister at a price that left a sizable hole in the Schwartzes' hard-earned savings. They sold their house and furniture-restoration business, and moved up to Johannesburg with Dawie—to make a new start in fresh surroundings, where

211

no one knew them. In parting from her son, Elsa had understood and accepted that she would never hear about or see him again. She had agreed with Mrs. Schwartz that there should be no further contact between them.

"But how could she bear it?" cried Lynn.

Behind the thick lenses of her glasses, Mrs. Schwartz's magnified eyes suddenly filled. "Because she loved him," she said, and left the table hurriedly.

Lynn looked wretched; I bowed my head to avoid her gaze. The congestion in my chest felt suffocating. A minute earlier, I had noticed the gold identity bracelet Mrs. Schwartz was wearing. The simple inscription read: *To Mum, Yours ever, Dave. 1975.*

Mrs. Schwartz was busy at the sink. It seemed to take her ages to fill the kettle and plug it in. She remained in the scullery, staring out of the small, burglar-barred window.

"Mrs. Schwartz . . . ?" Lynn's voice wavered. "Perhaps he'll come back."

The kettle started boiling. The figure at the sink didn't stir.

"Would you like us to go?" Lynn asked after a few moments.

"We'll have some more tea," Mrs. Schwartz said. She refilled our cups and sat down before she spoke again. "I also wanted the best for him. But more than anything else, I want Dawie—my Dave—to be happy. That's all I ask, for him to be happy. And maybe he will be happier now."

"Living as a Colored?"

Although it was Lynn who had asked the question, Mrs. Schwartz's eyes sought mine.

"Living as himself," she said. Then she reached out and touched the Star of David hanging on a chain round Lynn's neck. "As a Jew, you should understand," she told her. "In many places, many times, you couldn't wear this openly. For us Jews, anti-Semitism is a fact of life; like racism for Black people. My husband comes from Germany. The Nazis killed nearly all his family in the concentration camps."

"I'm sorry," Lynn said.

"One uncle managed to pass himself off as a Gentile, and he survived. Who could blame him? He had to think of his family. His wife wasn't Jewish. But they had two children. He saved them from the Nazis. They all survived the war. Then he killed himself . . . why?" she asked Lynn.

Lynn twitched uneasily. "Because he felt guilty?"

"Why, though? He had responsibilities to his family, and he had protected them. Other Jews who hid their identity during the war didn't all kill themselves afterwards. His wife loved him, but she couldn't stop him taking his own life. Why did he?"

"I don't know." Lynn was beginning to sound desperate.

Mrs. Schwartz shifted her attention to me. "Some people are maybe too sensitive and too hard on themselves. Loving them isn't enough to make them happy; you need to be able to change the world for them. But you can't change the world."

Her anguish was now plainly visible on her face. I could

213

only sit there helplessly, observing her pain as she continued.

"I have always been afraid for Dave because he was such a sensitive little boy. When he first came to us, he missed his mother—he missed Elsa very much, of course. He missed his sisters too. And his brother, Andries, though Andries was jealous of him, Elsa told me. I can see why. Elsa treated Dawie differently from her other children. She made him believe he was different. That was why he didn't question her decision to give him to us. He believed everything his mother told him. Small children are like that. He also believed White people are better than Colored people. But once he had accepted me as his mother, I *had* to tell him that White people aren't better than anyone else because I didn't want him to grow up into a racist. Being a very tenderhearted and intelligent and thoughtful little boy, he was, anyway, starting to discover that for himself, just by looking at what was happening around him. One day, after watching a police-dog display at the Rand Easter Show, he asked me why policemen liked black dogs but they didn't like Black people. Another day he asked me why White and Black people couldn't be friends and live together in one house. I had to try to explain to him about the laws of Apartheid. Young as he was, he could see the injustice of it all, and it disturbed him deeply. He didn't say much. He never said much, my Dave. He was a very internal child. But that night when I was putting him to bed, he clung to me and wouldn't let me go. And you know what he asked me? 'If I wake up Black in the morning, will you still love me, Mommie?' "

Mrs. Schwartz's face worked. She frowned in fierce concentration at the cold cup of tea she hadn't touched. Lynn put a hand over hers.

"I'd like to have seen him as a kid," she said. "I can just imagine how cute he was, with those beautiful big green eyes."

Mrs. Schwartz smiled up at her gratefully. "Naughty, too. He could be very naughty."

"I bet," said Lynn.

"I only wish, for his sake, he had turned out more like my Joseph, and was able to take life as it comes. But maybe it isn't possible for any pass-Whites to be at peace inside themselves. My son . . . Dave is not the only one, you know."

"I know," Lynn said. "Someone—actually it was my boyfriend—informed me last night that there are thousands of pass-Whites. *Thousands.* I had no idea. I'm so bladdy ignorant. The most terrible thing for them must be having to cut themselves off from their families. Joel—that's my boyfriend—was telling me about a guy, a pass-White, he knew of in Cape Town. The guy lived near his own mother and used to meet her quite often in the street on his way to work. But as he was usually with a White friend, he couldn't acknowledge her. He had to pretend he didn't recognize her—*his own mother!*"

Lynn's cheeks grew red in the silence that followed. Mrs. Schwartz had slumped back away from the table. I was scared to look at her. I felt as if I were going to choke, and clenched my teeth. The slow dripping of a leaking tap

215

in the scullery became a mental torture. I counted seven drips before Mrs. Schwartz spoke in a heavy, tired voice.

"I must trust to God to help him now, to let him be happy. He was never a happy boy. I know. Not in his heart. One part of him was happy, but another part, deep down, didn't ever believe it was right to have to hide what he was. For a while I believed he might be able to accept himself and make the most of the chances he had been given. It was what we all wanted for him, Elsa and Joseph and me, and—ya, Dave too. But not with his whole heart . . . ever. That was why he cut off his hair," she said, and paused.

I still couldn't look at her. The tap dripped twice. Then Lynn said, "I've been meaning to ask you—was his hair very frizzy? Is—"

"It wasn't very frizzy, just a little bit. Elsa used to straighten it, right from the time he was a young baby. She showed me how. You buy some special stuff. I needed to do it regularly. If I forgot, Dave would remind me. He hated it when it started to curl. But he had lovely hair. Soft and springy. I was heartbroken after he shaved it all off a few years ago."

She paused again. I cradled my head between my hands, hoping my face wouldn't be visible to her. Lynn's chair scraped on the floor.

"I don't—what possessed him, if it wasn't necessary?" Lynn asked.

"I think . . . maybe to understand someone, you have to know them very well, love them for a long time." I sensed she was addressing me directly now. "He said he got sick of having to take so much trouble over his hair,

216

keeping it straight. He said he preferred not to have to bother with it at all, *even if he looked funny, and people laughed at him*—which was the real reason, I knew. We didn't talk about it; he couldn't have talked about it. But I just *knew*. He *wanted* to look funny; he wanted to look obviously odd to everyone else and draw attention to himself. There was that part of him, deep down, pushing him to do it, wanting him to be found out as a pass-White."

"*Shit!*" Lynn exclaimed with uncontrollable feeling. "Joel is so *bladdy* right about this *bladdy* country!" Then she realized what she had said, and apologized abjectly for her language.

Mrs. Schwartz's response, if any, wasn't verbal. The room had fallen deathly quiet. I rubbed my eyes quickly and lifted my head. Mrs. Schwartz was staring at me. Her face had a set, faraway look, as if she weren't seeing me, but a vision of someone else sitting in my place.

"I was most frightened for him when he fell in love," she said. "We did have a long talk about this once, years ago, after he first started going out with girls. He was only thirteen or so at the time. And like all boys of that age—especially ones that don't have sisters to learn from—he was very ignorant about girls and unsure how to treat them." A wistful smile plumped out her soft cheeks. "He was sitting here in the kitchen, asking me all sorts of questions on the facts of life, and he got so embarrassed. We talked about love too. It was then he said he hoped he never met a girl he loved enough to want to marry, because if he did, he would have to tell her he was Colored—and he'd lose her, he said. I tried to reassure him. He was so vulnerable. I swore that if she was the right

217

girl, if she really loved him, it wouldn't make any difference to her feelings for him. 'And if we had a child, Mommie?' he asked me. 'It might be Black. We couldn't have a child, living here—could we?—even if we both wanted to.' How was I to answer that?" Her shoulders drooped. "I told him that the situation might be different in the country by then. . . . I prayed . . . I kept praying that it would be. . . ." She sank farther into her chair.

Had she been revengeful towards me, had she shouted at me, it might have been easier to bear than having to watch her pain turned in on herself. My lips moved soundlessly. I coughed, and my throat came unstuck.

"I think he tried to confide in me . . . a couple of times," I admitted. "But he obviously didn't trust my feelings sufficiently. And he was right."

Light glanced off her spectacles as she straightened up to gaze fully into my face. Her features were blurred by the tears I was holding back.

"You sound very chesty, my child," she said with concern. "You look like you have a temperature. You should go home. You need to be lying down."

"I'm all right." I gave her a wan smile. "Thank you . . . for explaining to me. I understand now why he never brought me here. He had to feel sure of me first, before introducing me to you."

She made a helpless gesture. "I'm glad you came today," she said, and stood up.

"Mrs. Schwartz . . . ?" My cheeks were wet; I wiped them on my arm. "I appreciate that you can't be expected to believe me, but I really do care about him. I love him.

218

I have to let him know. Will you tell me how to get hold of him?"

She made another gesture, indicating refusal. "You can come and see me again, though, if you want to. I'm always here." Then she laid a motherly hand on the top of my head. "Now you must go straight to bed and keep warm, so you don't catch a worse chill."

twenty-three

My cold turned into a bad flu. I was too ill to get out of bed for four days. Sophie and my mother looked after me. The house was unfamiliarly quiet with just the three of us in it. My father and Mark weren't due back from Durban before the middle of the week; my father had some business to do down there, and they were staying with his married sister—my aunt Edna, who had a son of Mark's age.

Sophie, predictably, laid the blame for my illness on my flight to and from Cape Town. As she explained: "You sit shut up in the airplane like Jonah in the belly of the big fish, Miss Rhonda. You can't breathe nicely. The air is no good. So you get sick—that's that."

Lynn came to visit me a couple of times. On her first

visit, she told me she had made up her mind to go and work on a kibbutz in Israel for a year. She had talked her father into agreeing to the idea and was anxious that the whole thing should be arranged as soon as possible.

"But what will you do about university?" I asked her.

"It'll have to wait. Right now it isn't my priority."

"And Joel?"

"I hope *he'll* wait. . . . Please God! He says he'll miss me, though he wants me to go. He reckons the experience will be good for me."

"Is that why you're going?"

"No, it was meeting Mrs. Schwartz that decided me." Glumly, she contemplated the jar of Vicks on my bedside table. "The truth is, Rhond, I'm not positive I want to be South African. I don't know if I can be an Israeli, but now is the time to find out. I have to give it a try." Her hand toyed with the six-pointed-star pendant, absently sliding it back and forth along its silver neck chain. "It's quite ironic, really. I guess I've discovered I've got an identity problem. . . . A bit like Dave," she mused. Then she looked into my face. "Rhond, have you worked out yet what you're going to do?"

I gazed at her dully. "Do?"

"About Dave?"

"Find him. I must *find* him—*somehow*."

I turned my head to cough and my nose started running. Lynn handed me the box of tissues.

"You're in a bad way," she sympathized. "Listen, I ought to push off now. I promised your ma I wouldn't stay long. She says you hardly slept at all last night, and you need all the rest you can get. But I'll pop in again tomorrow to see how you are. What can I bring you?"

"Books," I wheezed. "Would you ask Joel if he'd mind lending me a few of his books?"

"Which ones? He owns thousands."

"I noticed. I'd like to read whatever he's got on the history of Apartheid, and also any books written by Colored or Black South Africans. Do you think he'd mind?"

"Of course not. I'd better warn you, though, that a lot of the literature he has is banned."

"I'll be careful." I smiled feebly. "I'll read under the bedclothes."

"That's allowed. So long as they aren't *red under the bed*." She blew me a parting kiss. "I'll bring you as many as I can carry tomorrow."

She was as good as her word; and I spent the next two days reading, virtually without stop.

On Thursday I felt strong enough to leave my bed and sit in a chair at the window. A short while after lunch, my mother came in and found me crying. Lying facedown on my lap was a collection of essays and poems by a Black South African political exile. My mother glanced at the cover of the book, asked me if I was hurting anywhere, tested my temperature by pressing her palm to my cheek, tut-tutted over the food I hadn't eaten on the tray, and carried it away. Minutes later, she was back. This time she seated herself decisively at the end of the bed.

Clasping her hands round her knees, she said, "Rhonda . . . darling, please tell me what's making you so unhappy."

Only once before in my life had she spoken to me in this gentle, pleading manner. It was when I was seven and

222

I fell out of a tree. As I lay prone on the ground, half stunned, I had a muddled awareness of my mother's voice very close to my ear calling me "darling" and begging me to wake up. But I kept my eyes closed until my father arrived on the scene and lifted me into his arms. Eleven years later I still harbored a sense of guilt for having rejected her one open display of maternal demonstrativeness in my childhood.

The tree responsible for my fall was visible from the window. Bleary-eyed, I frowned at it indecisively, fighting with myself. When my mother, after waiting, moved to get up, my hand whipped out in a reflex action and restrained her.

"Mom! I'll tell you. Don't go. I'd like to be honest with you."

She sat down again.

While I explained about Dave, she listened in grave-faced silence, showing no emotion until I had finished. Then she surprised me by expressing genuine sympathy for him. "It must be terrible to be in his position," she said.

I hugged her. She patted me on the back, extricated herself, and offered me a fresh wad of tissues.

"Now give your nose a good blow. . . . That's better. You know, dear, it's probably just as well that it's happened. Things usually do turn out for the best in the long run. Of course, it's an awful shock. But imagine how much worse it would have been if you had gone on and married him, and only then found out that he was Colored."

"I want to marry him," I informed her.

I saw a flicker of fear in her eyes, yet she said confidently, "Naturally you're upset. I do understand, Rhonda. I know you were very keen on him. He *was* a nice lad. I liked him."

"*Was* a nice lad? He isn't dead." I felt as if *I* were dead inside and nothing mattered anymore except being with Dave again. "You mean he *is* a nice lad."

"Yes." She let herself smile. "There will be others, though, I promise you." Her hand patted my knee. "I remember when I was young how difficult it was to believe I would ever fall in love again, after the first time. But I did. And so will you, believe me. You'll meet lots of boys at university, and at the right moment the right one will come along and—"

"He already has," I said impassively. "I'm not getting through to you, am I? It isn't over between Dave and me. You talk as if I'm twelve, and he's my first boyfriend, and my feelings are pure puppy love. Well, they aren't. I'm in love with him, and I want him back—if he'll have me." I looked her fully in the face. "I think you should know that I've been sleeping with him, Mom. All that business about the Cohens, and staying in their flat at Clifton, was a lie. I lied to you. Dave and I spent two weeks in a hotel on our own."

As she recoiled, blanching, I suddenly saw a picture of myself as Dave must have seen me, huddled on the bed in Cape Town, horror-stricken at discovering I had had sex with a Colored—the expression on my mother's face was the expression Dave must have seen on mine. But my mother's paralyzing fear, I realized, was that I was pregnant. She seemed almost too terrified to ask the question. I watched her struggling to speak.

224

Then I told her, "I'm on the pill."

Her cheeks flushed with relief. "I suppose we can at least be thankful for *that*!" she said. She got up, straightened the bedclothes, and stalked out, leaving a decided chill in the air behind her.

She didn't come near my room for the rest of the afternoon. At teatime, she sent Sophie in with a glass of orange juice and a plate of biscuits. It was dusk by the time my father and Mark arrived home from their journey. I heard my mother and Sophie rush outside to welcome them. I remained where I was, in the chair beside the window, staring into the night.

I had shut my door earlier. My mother opened it and switched on the light.

"Your father's here," she announced. "What are you doing still out of bed?"

"Thinking," I said.

"You shouldn't be sitting in the dark like this, straining your eyes. And there's a draft. Can't you feel it?" She drew the curtains. "Are you sure you're warm enough?"

"Yes, thank you," I said.

"You've been coughing a lot. Did you take your medicine?"

"I did," I said.

"Your father will no doubt be in shortly to see you." She dithered, fidgeting with the bottles on the medicine tray. Then she dodged behind my chair. "If I were you, Rhonda, I wouldn't tell your father what you've told me."

My jaws clenched. "Why?" I asked.

"I just wouldn't." She was stooped over, her bottom sticking up in the air, remaking the bed. "It isn't necessary for him to know, and it would only upset him. When there's a suitable moment, I'll simply mention to him that you've . . . Where are you off to? . . . Rhonda . . . ?"

The study door stood slightly ajar. Through the opening, I glimpsed my father at his desk, reading his mail. I barged in.

"I need to talk to you, Dad. I would have waited, but I can't. Not now. It's too important. It's about Dave and me," I informed him, and launched into my explanation before I could lose my impetus.

He heard me out, sitting frozen in stillness. He appeared to be thunderstruck. Weak and sick with apprehension, I grinned at him nervously.

"Mom said I shouldn't tell you, but I wanted you to know because I—"

"Rhonnie . . . how could you . . . do this to me?" he whispered in an unrecognizable voice.

"Do what?" I croaked.

He shook himself, as if he were trying to clear his mind, and slumped forward over his desk. I noticed that the small bald spot at the crown of his head seemed to have become bigger during the past two weeks. A lump formed in my throat.

"Do what, Dad?" I implored him.

His fingers rifled through the pile of letters. "I've got to deal with *all* these, and I've had a *long* journey, Rhonnie, and I'm *tired*. We'll discuss it later."

Irresolute, I waited for him to raise his face. He didn't.

"All right, then," I said dispiritedly.

Something made me glance back after a few steps. He was sitting up, staring towards me. I had seen him wounded before, I had wounded him myself in the past, but never this badly—I had never seen him look this hurt before.

"Oh . . . Dad . . . !" I choked out.

"Why did you have to go to bed with him?" Tears brimmed his eyes.

"Have to? I didn't have to. Dad, I wanted to. I *love* him. *Please* understand."

He smiled sadly. "And you thought he loved you."

"He did love me," I corrected him. "I was the one who—"

"Love you?" he spluttered, growing purple in the face. "God Almighty, Rhonnie, if he had loved you, if he had respected you, he would have had the common decency to keep his filthy hands off you. He would have stuck to his own sort, not used you. But he won't get away with it. I'll have his—"

"Dad!" I said, horrified. "He didn't use me. What are you talking about?"

"The little swine set out to have sex with you because you're blond. His kind always go for blond White women—the blonder and whiter the better. They—"

"That isn't true." A deep sense of outrage triggered off a sudden fury in me. "That isn't true!" I yelled at him. "You know nothing about Dave's and my relationship. It wasn't just sex; what's more, *he* didn't persuade me to go to bed with him. For your information, *I* had to persuade *him* to—"

"I don't want to hear," he bellowed. "I'm not interested in listening to any of the lewd details, Rhonnie. I only hope to bloody hell he hasn't gone and got you pregnant and ruined your life even more than he already has done."

227

"Ruined my life? Is that really how you—"

"You'd have to have an abortion," he shouted me down, "and do you realize—"

"NEVER!"

I had succeeded in silencing him. He gaped at me. "I beg your pardon?"

"I wouldn't have an abortion."

"Are you out of your mind? You'd be carrying a Colored bastard child."

"I'd be carrying *Dave's* child, and I'd want to keep it."

"Like hell you would!" he exploded again. "You don't know what you're saying, unless for some reason you're— Rhonnie! are you deliberately trying to hurt me?"

"*Me?* . . . Hurt *you* . . . ?" I felt hysterical. My emotion gagged me, but I wrenched the words out somehow. "So much for your love, *and* your understanding. Mom was right. I shouldn't have spoken to you."

Wheeling round, I plunged away from him. He called after me. I responded by slamming the study door behind me.

Mark was in the passage. He fled into his bedroom at my appearance. I walked on to my room, turned, and walked back.

"You heard all that, did you, Mark?" I asked, striding to his bed, where he lay curled up against the wall.

He flapped an elbow by way of answer and tucked himself into an even tighter ball. Spoodie was chewing the remains of a pencil on the carpet. She wagged her tail at me guiltily. I leaned across the mattress and shook Mark's shoulder.

"Leave me alone," he muttered. "Jus' leave me alone!"

My fingers fastened round his shirt collar. I couldn't control my trembling.

"Sit up. Look at me," I said, and yanked him hard. He came unstuck. I heaved him upright and held him by the scruff of the neck. "Okay, so Dave is a Colored. So what? You liked him, and it shouldn't make any difference now to your feelings for him, should it?"

"How can he be Colored?" His childish treble quavered with shock. "He's as white as me."

Reminding myself that Mark was only nine helped to calm me down. More equably, I explained, "He is Colored, though, Markie; the rest of his family are all dark. His brother is very dark, like Sophie."

"Sophie?" I saw that he was appalled. "Sophie is a Black. You can't go out with a Black."

"Why not?" I asked, half anticipating the answer.

"Are you mad? Nobody goes out with a coon. You can't. I'd lose all my friends if you did."

I felt capable of wringing his neck. But I also knew I couldn't blame him. I would have reacted in much the same way at his age. In South Africa, one becomes a racist the day one is born.

I went back to my own room and locked the door.

twenty-four

Christmas was two days later. In keeping with custom, the family went to church in the morning. I refused to go with them. I stayed at home.

Over the traditional roast turkey dinner, laid out on the patio, Helen chose to make her announcement that she was expecting a baby. Victor looked very proud of himself. Mark pulled a sour face. My mother turned pink with pleasure and piled a second helping of vegetables onto Helen's plate. My father kissed Helen, thumped Victor's back, and opened a bottle of champagne to celebrate.

When Sophie came to clear away the dishes, my father gave her the good news. He offered her a glass of bubbly, and she knocked it back in three huge gulps. Then, to show her happiness for Victor and Helen, she performed a little dance; my father joined in, causing everyone to laugh. I left the table and went down to the bottom of the garden to be by myself.

Lolling on the bench in front of the tennis court, I tried to visualize what Dave was doing at that precise moment. I would have willingly exchanged all my worldly possessions for the chance to see him. In my mind, I spoke to him unhappily at some length. Helen interrupted my reverie.

"I've brought you a coffee, Rhonda."

She was carrying two cups, which meant she intended to have a chat. I inwardly cursed as she lowered herself carefully onto the bench.

"I put cream in it," she said. "I hope you wanted cream."

"Thanks," I murmured.

"You were awfully quiet at lunch."

"Was I?"

She scooped a spoonful of froth out of her cup and licked it. "Anyway, how do you feel about becoming an aunt?"

"I'm happy for you both."

"Ya?"

"Of course. It's what you've been wanting, isn't it?"

"More than anything in the world." She sighed.

"Then that's great. You're lucky." An ant was crawling up my ankle. I shook my leg, spilling my coffee. "Damn!" I said.

"Rhonda . . . you know, I . . . Mom told me you were taking it hard over your . . ."

My cup rattled on its saucer. "Over my what?"

"Your boyfriend."

"He has a name." I glared at her. "Mom told you all about it, did she? Trust her!"

"Don't be cross with Mom. It's all right to tell me. Hell, I'm your sister. And I wouldn't dream of breathing a word to anyone. The only reason I'm mentioning it now is because I want to say how sorry I am. I appreciate how you must feel."

"Do you?" I said.

"Listen, there's something I'd like to ask you. Victor and I have discussed it already, and I'd—we'd both love you to be our child's godmother." I hadn't been expecting this, and for an instant I was emotionally overwhelmed. She nudged my arm. "I hope you'll say yes, Rhonda."

"I wish I could," I replied after a pause.

"So what's stopping you?"

A large sulphur butterfly fluttered out of the shrubbery on my left. My eyes followed its meandering flight across the tennis court.

"We need to talk about it first, Helen." I swiveled round to face her. "You have to realize that I don't intend giving up Dave."

All the softness went out of her expression. "I'll never understand you," she said, hauling herself to her feet. "There's obviously no point in speaking to you until you've come to your senses. But I'm warning you"—she shook her finger in my face—"if you bring shame on the family, I'll disown you."

"Is that a promise?" I leered as she looked down her nose at me. "You're all heart, Helen," I said. She turned on her heel and strode up the lawn. "Thanks anyway— for the coffee," I called sarcastically.

232

A yellowish blob hurtled through the air towards her from behind me, landing in the grass a few inches from her right foot. She was in too much of a hurry to notice it. I wondered if it could possibly be the butterfly, but then Mark scrambled out of the shrubbery, clutching a slingshot.

"Missed! Blinking hell!" he moaned. "I was aiming for her bottom. I wasn't far off, though. I was pretty close. Did you see?"

"I saw," I answered disconsolately. "What was that yellow thing? Not a stone, I hope, Mark."

"Ag, just a bit of gem squash from the compost heap. It couldn't hurt her if it hit her." Straddling the bench, he sat swinging his legs. "Pity I missed. I'll have to practice more. This is a *lekker caty*.* I *smaak* it a lot. You know where I got it?"

"No," I said, uninterested.

"*Don't* you know?" He thrust the slingshot under my nose. "Dave made it for me. He carved it from a stick I found." Chewing his lip, he rubbed a thumb caressingly over the forked wood. His ears had gone bright pink. "Dave's ace, really."

Caustically, I said, "How very nice of you to admit it at last."

He scowled at me. "I *never* said I didn't *smaak* him, did I?"

"True enough. You *only* said you didn't want me to go out with him because he was a coon and you'd lose all your friends. That's *all* you said."

The rash of freckles across his cheeks disappeared be-

*terrific slingshot.

neath a red flush before he ducked his head. Drawing his knees up under his chin, he gave his minute attention to a newly healed scratch on his ankle. With a grimy fingernail, he picked at the scab.

"I never said that," he mumbled.

"Oh *yes* you *did!*"

"Well . . . I've changed my mind. You can go out with him. He and me are pals. You can marry him, if you like."

"How very generous of you, old chap." My facetiousness was a safety valve for my anger. "But what will all your precious friends think?"

"Nothing."

"*Nothing?* Are you *sure?*" I bullied him.

He poked his head up. His gaze narrowed in sullen defiance. "I won't tell them Dave's not White."

"I see. Only what you don't realize, Mark, is that Dave has decided to go back to living as a Colored, and I wouldn't bet on his being prepared to pass himself off as White now in front of your friends—just to please you! I wouldn't be so certain, either, that he even wants to continue to be your pal. He might feel the same way about you being White as you feel about his being Colored."

That gave Mark pause for thought; he hadn't taken the possibility into account. It hurt him. But he recovered quickly and made his face look mean.

"Too bad if he does. I couldn't care. I don't need Dave for a friend. I've got spans of friends," and he slithered off the bench and went away huffily.

My Christmas present from my father, a secondhand Volkswagen Golf, was parked on the pavement outside our house. In handing over the keys, my father had explained curtly, "It's your transport for university, Rhonnie." I had thanked him in a lukewarm manner. It was the first time we had spoken to each other since our row over Dave.

The car keys were lying in my room. I sneaked into the house, through the kitchen, to fetch them and the box of chocolates that I had bought and gift-wrapped the day before. On my way out, I stole a bottle of my father's expensive German white wine from the refrigerator. Nobody saw me depart. I didn't bother to leave a note to say where I was going.

Mrs. Schwartz hugged me warmly on the doorstep and led me by the hand into the front room to meet her husband. Straightaway I knew I would hit it off with him. He was small and bent but sprightly, with a neat, curly gray beard, wispy white hair, and crinkly, sharp blue eyes. He was also shy. He hardly spoke a word to me in the first half hour I was there, yet I didn't find his silence uncomfortable; he kept smiling at me while his wife and I chatted.

We drank a little of the wine I had brought. Then Mrs. Schwartz said that I must be hungry, and despite my assurances that I wasn't, she bustled out to the kitchen. Ranged along the mantelpiece were several framed photographs of Dave as a youngster. I was longing to go up close and study them, but I didn't like to do so in front of Mr. Schwartz.

He caught my eye. "Do you love our boy?" he asked bluntly.

"Yes," I said without hesitation.

He nodded, as if that had settled something for him.

"Can you play?" he asked next, gesturing towards the battered upright piano that took up a lot of space in the small room.

"Regrettably, no," I told him. "I had a few lessons once, but I never got the hang of it. Do you play, Mr. Schwartz?"

"Not Mr. Schwartz. Joseph," he corrected me. "I'll play. You sing. Ya?" He bounded agilely from his chair. "Come!"

"I can't sing," I protested, obediently following him to the piano.

He patted the stool. I sat down. He squeezed in beside me.

"What will you sing?" he asked.

My mind went blank. "I . . . don't know. You play for me first," I suggested.

He closed his eyes, resting his hands in his lap. They were large, heavy, muscular hands, the fingers thick and coarse, with chipped, grooved nails: the hands of a manual worker, not a musician. But when they flexed over the keyboard and tentatively felt out a chord, they seemed to lose their heaviness.

He played with his eyes shut. He had the sensitive touch of a blind person reading Braille; his fingers fluttered across the notes, appearing to barely press them. The simple melody was hauntingly sweet and sad. Abruptly, in the middle of a bar, his hands stilled.

"He isn't coming back here to live, you know," he said.

My heartbeat faltered.

"He rang this morning. He's made up his mind. He won't be going to university now, and he . . . I . . ." His voice gave out. Tears glistened in his eyes. He bowed low over the piano and thumped the keys hard. "Brahms is too sad," he rasped, trying to laugh. "We should sing something happy. Ya? . . . Something happy." Tremulous, his hands hovered uncertainly, then struck a few notes clumsily. "No, I forget . . . I can't play anymore today. Excuse me," he muttered, springing up. "I must blow my nose."

He hurried from the room, dodging past his wife, who had just entered with a loaded tea tray. I went to take it from her.

"Perhaps I shouldn't stay to tea," I said, avoiding looking her in the face.

"You have to stay. You have to eat my cookies and shortbread. We need to fatten you up. You're too skinny. You've lost too much weight since you were here last time. . . . Now you sit down," she ordered briskly, and I meekly obeyed her. She handed me a plate filled with goodies. "I want to see you finish all this."

To please her, I stuffed a biscuit in my mouth, chewed determinedly, and swallowed. The crumbs jammed my throat. I tugged my hair forward as my eyes filled up.

"My child . . ." Bending, she clasped me round the shoulders, drawing my head against her bosom. "My child. Never mind. We're all a bit sad today. It can't be helped. But it's good you came. I'm glad you did. Joseph's glad as well. I can tell. Don't worry about him. He's only upset right now because of talking to Dave on the phone this morning."

"I know; he said Dave had rung."

I was in control of myself again. She pinched my cheek lightly, fetched our cups of tea from the table, and settled herself in the chair next to mine.

"Mrs. Schwartz—how is he?" I burst out emotionally. "Dave, I mean. Is he happy?"

She lost her composure; for a brief second her face had the look of someone suffering a sudden stabbing pain. Then the spasm passed. She adjusted her spectacles, which had slipped down her nose.

"No, he isn't. How can he be happy at the moment?" she said, and gruffly brought me up to date on Dave's situation.

Apparently, not all the members of his family in Cape Town had welcomed him with open arms. Elsa had, of course; however, she intensely disapproved of his proposal to have himself reclassified as Colored and remain in Cape Town. That would spell the end of her long-cherished ambitions for him. She was adamant in wanting him to return to Johannesburg after the New Year, to finish his education, and forget all about her once more. She had said as much, tearfully, over the telephone to Mrs. Schwartz the previous evening.

"I assured her this was what Joseph and I wanted too, with all our hearts," Mrs. Schwartz informed me. "But I had to explain to her that I wasn't prepared to put pressure on Dave. It's a decision only he can make."

Then she told me that Dave's brother, Andries, had initially refused Dave entry into the family's house in the township. From a letter Dave had written to her, Mrs. Schwartz surmised that Andries was growing up very politically conscious and violently anti-White, and viewed

238

Dave as a turncoat, referring to him scornfully as "Whitey." Evidently, relations between the two brothers were still strained and causing a lot of tension and friction in the family.

"Whatever Dave decides to do," Mrs. Schwartz ended, on the verge of tears, "it will be difficult for him." She got up and took our empty cups to the tray.

"I thought he . . . Hasn't he decided?" I asked, hardly daring to hope.

She didn't turn round. She was doing something to her face with a handkerchief. After a silence, she said, in a gravelly voice, "I think he has. We'll have to wait and see."

From somewhere at the rear of the house, the sound of an electric saw started up. Mrs. Schwartz came back to her chair.

"That's my Joe in the shed. He's working with his wood. I was certain he'd be there. When he's upset, he always makes something, and it heals him. In a little while, he'll come for his tea, and he'll be his old self again." She spoke confidently, as if she wanted to reassure both of us. "My Joe isn't one to stay down for very long. . . . But aren't you going to have a taste of my shortbread?"

I broke off a bit and forced myself to eat it. Then I felt it was time I left, and stood up. Mrs. Schwartz saw me out. In the hallway, she asked if things were all right at home. The phrasing of her question was diplomatic; I knew, however, what she was really asking and I sensed her concern for me.

Feeling acutely ashamed, I said, "Not exactly. I've told my parents about Dave because . . . well, they liked him;

my mother and father both liked him. Now they . . ." I shrugged, blushing with humiliation. "I'm afraid they're typical White South Africans."

"I'm sorry." She took my hand and pressed it between hers. "So it can't be easy for you at home. Never mind. I suppose they think they're trying to protect you because they love you."

My eyelids were prickling. "They *believe* they love me, like I *believed* I loved Dave," I said bitterly. "It isn't worth very much, though, is it, that sort of love without understanding. Not when it's put to the real test."

As I went forward to open the door, she dropped the bombshell:

"You can see him next Saturday," she said quietly behind me. "He'll be here then. He's coming up from Cape Town to fetch his motorbike."

I literally flew at her; my hug almost knocked her off her feet. "Thank you!" I cried. Then I was suddenly terrified and dubious. "But will he see me?"

She shrugged, looking a bit doubtful herself. "I don't know. I hope so. You've proved to me now that you care about him. Maybe there is still a chance for you two. I would like to think so."

"If there is—if I can persuade him—would it hurt you very much if he and I went away overseas?" I asked her.

She smiled. "We'll cross that bridge when we get to it. I'll expect you in the morning on Saturday. Good-bye, my child. Safe journey."

She waved me off from the veranda. I drove the length of the block, with the car bucking and backfiring, before I noticed the hand brake was on.

twenty-five

He stood against the mantelpiece with his arms folded. After the brilliant sunshine outside, my eyes had to adjust to the relative darkness inside the room. But I sensed, in that first instant, his hostility, and my veneer of confidence crumbled.

Idiotically, I stuttered, "H-happy N-new Year, Dave."

As I spoke, he started forward. My heart skipped a beat.

"You haven't closed the door," he said, and he brushed past me to close it himself. Then he walked over to the other side of the room.

He looked very different. He was growing his hair! The new growth was hardly more than a stubble at this stage, but it dramatically enhanced his attractiveness; my heart missed a second beat.

Perching on the narrow windowsill, he frowned at the locket hanging from its chain outside my blouse. "You might as well sit down," he suggested unenthusiastically.

I remembered the large envelope tucked under my arm, and went to hand it to him.

"This is from Mark. I don't know what it is. He wouldn't tell me," I explained.

While he slit open the envelope and extracted its contents, I hovered, quaking inside. He bent his head. In the brightness of the light coming through the window, his hair was a warm oatmeal color; my palms itched to feel it and discover the texture. I stabbed my nails into them sharply.

"It's Spoodie." He let out a chuckle. "Mark has sent me a picture of Spoodie." He held it up.

My little brother possessed no talent whatsoever for drawing. Nevertheless, he had clearly taken a lot of trouble over this particular attempt at a crayon portrait—as the countless smudged eraser marks proved. The anatomy of the subject more closely resembled a shaggy sausage on four stilts than a live dog; however, the necessary clues to its identity were provided by the coloring and the over-long, feathery tail. Above the drawing, in bold, uneven lettering, was printed the message: *To Dave, Happy New Year from Mark, and Happy New Licks from Spoodie.* Underneath, a hastily scribbled P.S. had been added, which I couldn't read because the sheet of paper was no longer steady in Dave's hand.

I glanced up and met the unguarded gaze of gold-green

eyes. Their expression fired me with a sudden exultant certainty. I had so much to say to him, only I was totally inarticulate now. And so, it appeared, was he. With his face full of pain, he just looked at me helplessly.

"I love you," I got out at last. "Please, Dave, forgive me. Please, can't we try again?"

The need to touch him, to hold him, was tearing me apart. But the first move had to come from him. His hand began to reach out. Then he seemed to collect himself. Hunching his shoulders, he leaned right back against the window, away from me. His face went hard.

"You shouldn't be here. There's no point," he said. "It's over between us."

"It isn't—it doesn't have to be," I cried, almost begging. "So long as we love each other. That's all that counts. Nothing else matters."

"Love?" A skeptical smile twisted the left side of his mouth. "What exactly do you mean by that word? Do you mean you're prepared to move down to Cape Town?"

"If you'd like me to, yes. I could go to Cape Town University, and at least we'd be near each other and—"

"Not near enough. Or are you also prepared to dye your hair, and have a frizzy perm, and blacken your face, and live as a so-called Colored? Mind you, I doubt you'd pass very successfully. You're transparent White—especially when you blush."

My cheeks and neck were burning; I was momentarily stunned by his sarcasm.

"Now do you give up?" he taunted. "Now do you see that it can't work?"

"No." I raised my chin stubbornly. "I've some money.

We could emigrate. Obviously there's too much against us in South Africa. We need to leave it all behind. We could go to London and start—"

"You think we can leave it *all* behind?"

"If we—"

"You think we can leave ourselves behind, do you?"

I frowned, uncertain of his meaning. He waited a moment.

Then he said, "You must be bloody naïve if you believe it's possible for us to be completely natural with each other now. Never mind there being too much against us, there's too bloody much between us." He made an angry gesture. "Our relationship has—we've lost our color blindness. So what's the point? You and I . . . it just won't work. Why can't you see that for yourself?"

I couldn't see it. All I could see, in my emotional shock, was that I had failed to win him round. He had said we were finished, and he meant it; the confirmation was in his face.

"All right, tell me what *you* want."

His eyes stared into mine, weighing, measuring. Grimly, he said, "What I want is quite simple, really. I want to be me. I don't want to *have* to be either a so-called White or a so-called Colored. I want to be only me—unclassified. It's my ambition: to live a life in which I'll be judged by my own merits, not by the amount of pigmentation in my skin. And at last I've decided to get off my backside and do something about it."

"Do what?" I asked in trepidation.

"I can't tell you. That would be giving too much away." He shrugged. "Let's just say I'm being politically educated. My brother, Andries, is a damn good teacher. He's helped me sort out my priorities." Gathering himself up, he glanced pointedly at the door. "Listen, I think you'd better go now. I have to work on my bike. It's developed an oil leak."

"Yes," I said dully. Then my pride let me down; hot tears scalded my eyes. "I'm sorry," I bleated, "but I . . . must know—will I see you again? Can we at least keep in contact?"

"No."

He wouldn't look at me. He was folding up Mark's drawing. I saw that his hands were shaking.

"Dave!" I cried out.

"No—NO! . . . Just GO, will you?" he said violently.

I stumbled blindly over the floor, knocking into furniture. I had got as far as the door when he called to me to wait. I spun round.

"Rhonda, I love—" He caught his breath. "Give Mark my love."

Desolate, choking, I gazed at him hopelessly across the room. And then I went out.

epilogue

I haven't seen Dave for three years. *Three years.* I'm now
a university graduate. And I'm *still* in South Africa. It's
quite ironic, really, that since I've changed my mind about
leaving the country, so has my father. He has been pres-
suring me to study for my Master of Arts at a British
university. He obviously disapproves of my organizational
role in students' anti-Apartheid protests, but that isn't the
main cause of his change of heart. He is terrified that
sooner or later I'm going to be arrested by the security
police, and he wants to get me out of harm's way by
sending me overseas. I intend, however, to stay here and
continue my studies at Wits.

Why? The answer is difficult to explain. In some in-
definable way, I have become emotionally bound to South

Africa through my relationship with Dave. I feel a personal involvement with my country, and a deep indignation at the inhumanity of the system governing it.

I haven't yet got over Dave, if I ever will. He is with me all the time. When I walk down the street, I see him in the faces around me. I see him in Black faces, White faces, Colored faces. I find I look at Black people differently now; in the past I used to look at them without really seeing them.

Again, it's ironic: My father is afraid for me, and I'm afraid for Dave. I live in daily dread of a telephone call from Mrs. Schwartz to say he has been killed. She shares my fear. Dave writes to her regularly: loving, carefully worded letters that diligently omit to tell her what he is up to. But she knows what he is up to. She and I both know that he has dedicated himself to the Black liberation struggle. Several months ago, his brother, Andries, was shot dead when a large group of demonstrators clashed with the police in one of Cape Town's Colored townships. It wasn't an isolated incident; sporadic outbreaks of violence have become a common feature of life in non-White townships all over the country. But since then, Dave's letters guardedly hint at a hardening of his political resolve. Reading between the lines, one can detect a growing bitterness and anger in him that make us fear all the more for his safety.

On my worst days, I feel envious of Wendy. She won an art scholarship and went to Paris, to study at the Sorbonne. I receive the odd postcard from her. She sounds very happy. Helen is also happy. She and Victor have a chubby, pink-cheeked daughter and are expecting a second baby. Helen and I no longer talk to each other. She believes I've become a traitor to my own country. By "country" she means, of course, the privileged life-style of the White minority. My mother believes, or tries to believe, that my interest in politics is an unfortunate phase I'll grow out of. No doubt she blames it on my hormones and is secretly praying I'll fall in love with a nice, steady, conventional young man who'll straighten me out. Mark, too, is hoping (vainly) that I'll get married, so he can take over my room. He has developed a passion for computers and won't think or talk about anything else.

As far as the subject of marriage goes, at least I can feel happy for Lynn and Joel. Lynn spent a year and a half in Israel and then came back. And now she and Joel are engaged and planning to marry soon. I see a lot of them. We're all involved in the same anti-Apartheid organization. The organization isn't banned—as yet—although a number of its leaders, including Joel, have received visits from the Special Branch.

So much for the present. The future? I don't know. At times I am hopeful. At times I despair. What is certain is that the edifice of Apartheid is currently undergoing considerable alterations. Opinions differ as to the significance. Some political moderates claim that the whole Apartheid structure is beginning to be dismantled, at a piecemeal rate necessary to allay White fears and prevent chaos and economic collapse. Political radicals counterclaim that the architecture is merely being redesigned to provide Apartheid with a more acceptable façade to the outside world.

Recently, the constitutional change giving limited parliamentary power to Coloreds and Indians was disclaimed by a huge percentage of the people in both groups because it denied similar political rights to the African majority. (Neither Mrs. Schwartz nor I have any doubt that Dave was among those who denounced it.) Now the government has decided to abolish the two heinous laws banning sex and marriage across the color bar. In my view, this does clearly represent a significant reform, although it doesn't necessarily spell the end of Apartheid. Residential, educational, and social segregation remain entrenched in the Group Areas Act. What this new reform simply means is that couples like Dave and me will now be made exempt from certain conditions of the Group Areas Act as it applies to the rest of the population. However, it is a start; it might even prove to be a first real crack in the Apartheid foundation. It's hard to tell at this stage.

If I could, I would marry Dave tomorrow; without my parents' approval, which I know they wouldn't give despite the law being now on my side. But I can't believe that I will ever see Dave again. After three years I've finally stopped dreaming of him turning up unexpectedly on my doorstep.

Sometimes I lose track of what I'm fighting for. Yesterday evening, a militant African acquaintance informed me categorically that White politics had become irrelevant. Meaningful change, he asserted, would only be achieved now through the concerted action of the Black multitude. During the night, I dreamed Dave was dead. This morning, I woke up listless and depressed. When I arrived at university, Lynn greeted me with the news that the Special Branch had paid Joel another visit. I left the campus and walked to a nearby café in Braamfontein to have a cup of coffee on my own.

I was despondent, scared, ready to throw in the towel. My coffee looked like muddy river water. But I drank it and ordered a second cup.

The next table was occupied by two attractive, well-dressed girls in their late teens, one of whom had long blond hair. They were talking so loudly, I couldn't avoid overhearing their conversation. The blonde worked in a lawyer's office. She was regaling *telling* her friend with the disturbing details of a pending divorce case, involving a White couple who had produced a Black child. The husband, apparently, was to blame; it had been discovered that there was Colored blood in his family, which he hadn't even known about. The wife was now suing him for divorce. The two girls seemed to find the whole situation amusing. They were convulsed in giggles.

"But what will happen to the child?" the friend thought to ask at last.

"I dunno. The ~~woman~~ *mother* doesn't want it, obviously. I mean, would you? . . . Hey, look at the time. Have you finished? We must hurry, or I'll be late."

My eyes followed the blonde out of the café. From the back, she could have been mistaken for me. I saw in her an image of myself four years ago.

The confusion cleared suddenly from my mind. My irresolution was gone. I perceived very clearly what I was fighting for. I got up to pay my bill.

Outside, it had started to rain, but the sun was shining in a blue patch of sky: a monkey's wedding. I paused on the sidewalk. Smiling, with my face turned up to catch the cooling splashes, I wondered if it was also raining in Cape Town.

250